"I'm not going to hurt you. I came here to save you. You have to believe me."

He lifted a hand to touch her cheek. "You know me," he murmured.

Her whole body tingled at the contact. For the longest time, she stood with her eyes closed, drinking him in.

She did know him. There was something so thrillingly familiar about the touch of his hand, the sound of his voice. The way he looked at her.

Just then, the front door flew open and she screamed.

Instantly, he leaped in front of her, putting himself between her and the icy wind that swept through the cabin.

And in that moment, Claudia had no doubt that if a gunman had sto[illegible] in the doorway, Jack Maddox would ha[illegible] bullet for her.

AMANDA STEVENS

MAGNUM FORCE MAN

TORONTO • NEW YORK • LONDON
AMSTERDAM • PARIS • SYDNEY • HAMBURG
STOCKHOLM • ATHENS • TOKYO • MILAN • MADRID
PRAGUE • WARSAW • BUDAPEST • AUCKLAND

Special thanks and acknowledgment to Amanda Stevens for her contribution to the Maximum Men miniseries.

Recycling programs for this product may not exist in your area.

ISBN-13: 978-0-373-69436-5

MAGNUM FORCE MAN

This edition published by arrangement with Harlequin Books S.A.

www.eHarlequin.com

Printed in U.S.A.

ABOUT THE AUTHOR

Amanda Stevens is a bestselling author of more than thirty novels of romantic suspense. In addition to being a Romance Writers of America RITA® Award finalist, she is also a recipient of awards for Career Achievement in Romantic/Mystery and Career Achievement in Romantic/Suspense from *RT Book Reviews* magazine. She currently resides in Texas. To find out more about past, present and future projects, please visit her Web site at www.amandastevens.com.

Books by Amanda Stevens

HARLEQUIN INTRIGUE

759—SILENT STORM*
777—SECRET PASSAGE*
796—UNAUTHORIZED PASSION†
825—INTIMATE KNOWLEDGE†
834—MATTERS OF SEDUCTION†
862—GOING TO EXTREMES
882—THE EDGE OF ETERNITY
930—SECRETS OF HIS OWN
954—DOUBLE LIFE
1035—TEXAS RANSOM
1143—SHOWDOWN IN WEST TEXAS
1169—MAGNUM FORCE MAN

*Quantum Men
†Matchmakers Underground

CAST OF CHARACTERS

Claudia Reynolds—When an enigmatic stranger turns up out of the blue, claiming he's been sent to save her, Claudia's first instinct is to send him packing. But how can she discount his outrageous claim when he's able to foretell her every move?

Jack Maddox—He knows only one thing: he must find the woman and save her.

Red—A sadistic killer with a terrifying agenda.

Kenneth Sykes—A genetic research scientist who likes to play God.

Red, Blue and Green—Sykes's genetically altered enforcers.

Bill Elliot—A dedicated FBI agent investigating a series of kidnappings that appear to be tied to Sykes.

Chapter One

He knew three things. His name was Jack Maddox. There was somewhere urgent he needed to be. And the woman had to be saved.

Beyond that, he only *felt*. The icy rain pricking his face. The heaviness of his fatigued muscles. The pervasive fear that chilled him to the bone. Not so much for himself, but for the woman.

Whoever she was. Wherever she was.

He had to find her before they did.

Whoever they were.

His sodden clothing was like a lead weight as he stumbled through the dripping forest. He didn't know how much longer he could keep going. He needed rest, food, sleep. It seemed as if he'd been running forever. Running from something and to someone.

But who? *Who?*

Keep going. Don't stop until you get there. You'll know it when you see it. You'll know her.

The picture in his mind was that of a tall, slender

brunette with wide, knowing eyes. But it was only a vague impression. Her features were indistinct because his mental photograph kept changing. The one thing that remained the same, however, was the aura of danger that surrounded her. If he didn't find her in time, they would kill her.

Whoever they were.

He slowed for a moment to catch his breath, and that was a mistake because exhaustion swooped down like a vulture, picking away at the last of his resolve. He could lie down right there in the freezing rain and fall asleep. Maybe sleep forever.

The temptation was a little too seductive so he forced himself to push on.

But in that brief respite, he'd allowed other images to seep into his numb brain. Dark, endless passageways. Metal bars blocking every exit. The sting of a thousand needles.

As the hazy memories bombarded him, he tripped and fell to one knee, then sprang up with a renewed sense of purpose. He would never go back there. Never.

Wherever there was.

He had no idea how long he'd been on the run, but judging by his fear and urgency, freedom was a new experience. So new that when a thunderbolt cracked overhead, he flinched and ducked, then braced himself for the red-hot sear of a bullet ripping through his flesh. Instead, he smelled burning wood and ozone where lightning had struck a nearby tree.

He kept moving.

On and on through the woods until up ahead, in a flash of lightning, he saw the glimmer of wet pavement. He'd found the road. He had no real recollection of it, but he recognized it just the same. He also knew that he'd never physically been there before.

Winding like a silver ribbon through the craggy hills, the glistening pavement beckoned. With an almost hypnotic obedience, he came out of the trees and stood gazing in first one direction, then the other.

Which way?

Over the pounding rain and roaring thunder, another sound penetrated. A car engine coming up on his left.

He turned his head to watch the road as he huddled inside his wet clothing. He was so cold. He couldn't remember a time when he hadn't been chilled. He could barely even imagine what it must be like to feel warm and safe. Had he ever experienced either of those things?

Had he ever experienced...anything?

He felt curiously empty. Blank, like a chalkboard that had been erased, leaving only faint traces of what had been there before. And even those blurred markings would soon disappear as new information was imprinted upon the surface.

Had his memory been erased? Had new information been imprinted over the images of his past? Was that why everything in his mind was so muddled?

What about the woman? Did she even exist outside his head?

She *had* to exist because at that moment she seemed to be his only reason for being.

The hum of the engine grew louder and now he could see a faint glow from the headlights, but the vehicle was still hidden by a sharp curve in the road.

He waited.

Some instinct told him he should step away from the shoulder, but he didn't. *Couldn't.* He was glued to that very spot by destiny, fate or perhaps by something he didn't yet understand. All he knew was that he could not have moved if his life depended on it.

Rain slashed across his face as the drum rolls of thunder drew nearer. Like a celestial portent, streamers of lightning exploded across the midnight blue sky, and the wind in the trees behind him began to howl. The night was wet, cold, electric. And yet something inside him had gone still and pensive, his senses on hyper-alert, as if waiting for a silent command, an unheard voice assuring him that all would be well.

"Where are you?" he whispered to the wind.

No answer. No command. No warning. No anything. He was on his own.

The vehicle rounded the curve, and suddenly the cold and fear vanished, overridden by a keen sense of excitement and a certainty of what he now had to do.

As the headlights cut a swath through the blurry darkness, he walked into the middle of the road and turning, put up his hands to halt the oncoming vehicle.

Chapter Two

The road was a narrow tunnel carved between two black walls of spruce and cedar. Even on clear nights, the light was all but shut out by the overhanging branches, limiting visibility to the reach of the high beams. Tonight, except for the flashes of lightning that penetrated the evergreen canopy, it was like motoring through a deep canyon.

Even so, Claudia Reynolds wasn't particularly concerned. She'd driven under much poorer conditions and there wasn't another soul on the road. In another twenty minutes, she'd be home, safe and sound, sipping a cup of tea in front of a toasty fire—

The shadow that darted onto the road in front of her took her by surprise, and she reacted on pure instinct. Her foot came down hard on the brake pedal as she swallowed a scream. The car went into a mad skid as the rear careened wildly.

For what seemed an eternity, Claudia pumped the brakes and fought the wheel as the vehicle skated uncontrollably across the wet pavement toward the row of trees at the shoulder.

Somehow she got the vehicle straightened and stopped, and in the silent aftermath of near catastrophe, her heartbeat sounded as loud as the thunder.

She sat for a moment, still gripping the wheel, paralyzed with dread as her racing pulse kept time with the windshield wipers. Had she hit him?

No! She couldn't have. There would have been an impact.

Oh, God, maybe there had been an impact. Maybe in all the excitement, she hadn't noticed. Or maybe she just didn't want to believe it.

She closed her eyes and drew a shuddering breath as she sat there listening to the tick of the cooling engine. She would have to get out and look.

Her heart dropped to her stomach because it was the exact scenario that would have had her screaming at the ill-fated characters in the scary movies she used to devour. Now that her own life had become such a horror show, Claudia didn't enjoy the classic slasher flicks nearly as much as she once had.

She could almost hear herself yelling at the hapless heroine: *Don't get out of the car, you idiot! He's only pretending to be hurt!*

For all she knew, he could be one of them. The men who hunted her so ruthlessly.

Claudia knew only one by sight, the sadist who had brutally tortured and murdered her mentor in Chicago two years ago. She'd caught nothing more than a glimpse of his face a split second before the elevator doors closed, but his red hair, so incongruent with such a dark visage, and those cold, soulless eyes still haunted her sleep.

That nameless killer and the covert organization he worked for were the reasons she'd fled her home in the middle of the night and sought refuge deep in the heart of the Black Hills of South Dakota.

On good days, she almost managed to forget they were still out there somewhere looking for her, but then something like this would bring it back and she would be reminded all over again of their evil objective. She would be bombarded by the images of their brutality and the gruesome knowledge of how horribly Dr. Lasher had suffered before he died. How she would suffer if they ever found her.

What if the man in the road had been sent by that deadly cabal to find her? What if his intent was to torture her for information and then kill her? After all her meticulous preparations, she'd be a fool to fall into such an obvious trap.

Why, oh why had he run out in front of her like that? Hadn't he seen her headlights?

Leave him! Just drive away and don't look back!

But what if he was just an unlucky motorist whose car had broken down in the middle of a storm and he'd been trying to flag her down for assistance? Maybe he was hurt or sick and that was why he'd acted so erratically.

Not your problem. What kind of lunatic would deliberately step in front of an oncoming car, especially at night in a hard, driving rain?

The dangerous kind, Claudia's brain kept insisting.

All of this flashed through her head in the space of a heartbeat. Already she was reaching for her bag.

First, she checked her cell phone even though she knew she wouldn't get a signal. She rarely got one so far from town, which was why she'd also had a land line installed in the cabin.

Next, she grabbed a flashlight from the glove box and removed the small Ruger she kept hidden beneath her front seat.

As she felt the weight of the stainless-steel revolver in her hand, she registered the irony even as she expertly checked the chamber. She'd always hated guns. Even in her dangerous neighborhood back in Chicago, she'd never once contemplated arming herself because the gun culture mentality was abhorrent to her.

But finding Dr. Lasher's mutilated body had changed and toughened her after she'd had time to get over the shock. She'd been forced to open her eyes to the brutal reality of her situation. On the run, she'd quickly come to the realization that if she were to survive, she'd have to learn to take care of herself because she had no one else in her life who could protect her. No one.

Her keenly hewn survival instinct should have kept her at home this night, but when she'd left the house earlier, the dark clouds hovering over the hills had still seemed a long way off. With supplies running low and a bad case of cabin fever, she'd ignored the warnings, braved the weather and driven into Rapid City where she'd seen a movie, had an early dinner and stocked up on enough groceries to last her a couple of weeks.

As she'd driven out of town, the storm still hadn't unduly concerned her. Her small SUV had four-wheel drive, the road to the cabin was in good shape and her night vision was excellent. Nothing at all to worry about except for a man running out into the middle of the road in front of her.

Bracing herself, Claudia opened the door and climbed out, then went wide so that she would have a clear view of the front of the vehicle. She could see the silent form in front of the headlights. He lay right beneath her left bumper. And he wasn't moving. At all.

Rain pummeled her face as she eased toward him. Tightening her fingers around the grip of the revolver, she stood over him for a moment, gathering her courage before kneeling beside him to check for a pulse. He was alive. Unconscious but most definitely alive.

She ran the flashlight beam over him. She couldn't tell if he'd been hit, but she saw no evidence of gushing wounds or broken limbs. Thank goodness for that. Still, there could be internal injuries or a head wound that might not reveal itself until later...until it was too late.

Shuddering at the possibilities, she bent lower. His wet face was turned toward her and she could see raindrops shimmering on his lashes and in his dark hair. He looked young, probably not much older than her own twenty-four years. His angular face was shadowed but unlined, and Claudia found something heart-tuggingly innocent about his features, about his present vulnerability.

Tearing her gaze from the unconscious man, she rose and glanced around. They were miles from anywhere. What on earth was she supposed to do with him?

She wouldn't be able to call the police or an ambulance until she got back to the cabin, and maybe not even then if the storm had knocked out the phone lines. It could be hours or even days before service was restored. She could go for help, but with the temperature dropping, he might freeze to death before she made it back.

Pulling her parka tightly around her, she shifted indecisively in the cold rain. She hated to admit it, but there really was only one thing she could do. She had to drive him back to Rapid City. Self-preservation had consumed her for two whole years, but even she wasn't single-minded enough to leave an unconscious man stranded in a rainstorm.

Yet when she thought about the trail of gore that had led her to Dr. Lasher's mutilated body in the lab, her heart started to flail even harder. She didn't like this setup. It seemed too staged. Like an ambush.

That notion caused her to glance around anxiously, her eyes peering through the wet darkness for any sign of movement as she listened for the slightest sound. But all was quiet except for the rain pelting the pavement and the hood of the car. And the stranger's face. She needed to get him inside. He was already drenched. If he didn't die of exposure or internal injuries, he might succumb to pneumonia.

Hurrying back around to the door, Claudia climbed inside the SUV and rummaged in the glove box yet again, this time for a roll of duct tape. It was on every survivalist's short list, and she'd made sure to stock up when she first moved to the woods.

Returning to the unconscious man, she slipped the revolver into her coat pocket, then secured his wrists and ankles with the tape.

Mindful of any possible injuries, she took as much care as she could in moving him, but a certain amount of manhandling was necessary just to get him around to the door.

The old Claudia had been something of a couch potato, but Fugitive Claudia followed a strenuous workout routine to keep in peak form. Despite her fitness and the man's lean frame, however, dragging an unconscious body in a freezing downpour was not exactly a piece of cake.

After several minutes of pushing and prodding and hoisting, she finally managed to get him inside the vehicle. Winded, she climbed over the back of the seat and got behind the wheel. She was shivering so badly she took a moment to compose herself as she turned up the heat and put the gun within easy reach.

At least with his hands and feet secured, he wouldn't be able to catch her by surprise.

That was her hope, at least.

It took forever to turn the vehicle on the narrow road. Taking her time, she backed toward the wall of trees, eased forward over fallen twigs and leaves, then reversed again inch by slippery inch. Even with every precaution, though, she skirted too close to the edge and the rear tires slid off the pavement, spun uselessly for a heart-stopping moment before once again finding purchase.

A groan from the backseat snapped her head around, and she switched on the interior light to check on her unwelcome passenger. He lay on his back, eyes closed, his face ghostlike in the harsh glare.

"You okay?"

Nothing. Not so much as an answering whimper.

"Hey, you."

Still no answer.

"Who are you?" she wondered aloud.

And why am I doing this? Why, why, why?

The painstaking maneuvering had kept her on pins and needles, but once she had the vehicle turned and headed back toward town, she breathed a little easier. The sooner she could dump the stranger at the hospital where he'd receive proper medical attention, the better.

'Dump' might be a harsh word, but she had no intention of lingering any longer than was necessary. Ever since she'd arrived in Rapid City, Claudia had made a point of keeping a low profile, though she didn't try to make herself invisible.

To the contrary, she drove into town every few days to shop, dine out and go to a movie. She didn't want the locals to think of her as a recluse because that could also draw unwelcome attention and speculation. The trick was to seamlessly blend in, and up until tonight, she'd managed to do a pretty credible job. But the unconscious stranger in her backseat now threatened to throw a monkey wrench into her carefully scripted life.

Nothing she could do about that tonight. All she could do was get him to a doctor and hope for the best.

Fog crept over the windows, and Claudia switched the heater to defrost. Not that it would help much with the visibility. The rain was coming down so hard, she could barely make out the road in front of her and the lightning strikes were getting closer. A little too close, judging by the blast of thunder directly overhead and the static electricity that tingled her scalp.

As she rounded a curve, she caught a glimpse of something else in the road. Not a body this time, but a downed tree. Lightning had split a giant spruce endways, cleaving it cleanly in two so that one vast trunk came down across the road while the other side smashed back into the forest. Claudia braked and sat for a moment, gazing through the windshield at the tangled black mass of heavy limbs and leaves, still glittering and dripping with raindrops.

She had a rope in the back of the SUV, but the splintered trunk was so huge she wasn't at all sure her engine had enough power to pull it out of the way. And that was assuming she could tie a knot tightly enough to hold. All she might succeed in doing was overheating the motor, and then they'd be stuck here indefinitely.

So what were her options?

The man stirred in the back seat and she glanced nervously over her shoulder. She still didn't like this situation. Not one bit. Alone with a stranger was not how she'd planned to spend the rest of her evening. What if he *was* a killer?

The hair at the back of her neck rose, not from static electricity, but from pure, unadulterated fear. Her hand crept to the gun on the seat beside her. She knew how to use the weapon. She'd made certain of that. And since his wrists and ankles were bound, she definitely had the upper hand.

So why was she sitting there paralyzed by fear?

This was no good. She had to do something. She couldn't stay out on the road all night. If she stalled the engine or ran out of gas, they'd both freeze to death. Not to mention be sitting ducks.

She drew a quick breath. *Okay, focus. Make a decision and live with it.*

But the dripping chaos in front of her had made the decision for her. With the road blocked, she couldn't get the stranger to a hospital, and if she took him back and left him where she'd found him, he'd likely freeze to death. And that she couldn't live with because he might be just some poor guy down on his luck.

And, too, Claudia couldn't be absolutely certain the bumper had missed him. If her vehicle had struck him, she was somewhat responsible for his safety even though the idiot *had* been standing in the middle of the road.

Serve him right if I did kick him out.

But even as she grumbled to herself, she was already backing up and carefully turning the vehicle yet again on the slippery road.

"Do not make me regret this," she muttered as she shot another anxious glance over her shoulder.

Chapter Three

Twenty minutes later they were home.

The electricity was off so Claudia had to get out in the storm and manually unlock and raise the garage door. Hurrying inside, she checked the phone for a dial tone, but just as she'd feared, the line was dead.

Dammit!

Nothing was going her way tonight. If she were the superstitious type, she might think there was a bit of divine intervention working against her, but she had enough real problems to worry about. Like having a cold-blooded killer on her trail. Like dealing with an unconscious stranger in her backseat. She didn't exactly need to manufacture drama.

Going back out to the garage, Claudia positioned the flashlight to allow the beam to illuminate a trail back into the house. Then she wrestled the stranger out of the vehicle and onto the garage floor.

"Hey." She knelt beside him and slapped his cheeks

to try and bring him around. "Come on, wake up. I'm gonna need a little help here."

His lids fluttered open and he looked up at her. Claudia wasn't sure if it was the way the light hit his eyes or her own fanciful imagination, but his gaze seemed to have an unnatural glow. Otherworldly and completely devastating. She sat back on her heels, gobsmacked by the impact of that stare.

With some effort, she rallied her composure. "Hey, can you hear me? We need to get you inside. I'm going to take the tape off your ankles so you can walk, okay? But I'm warning you…don't try anything. I have a gun and I'm fully prepared to use it."

She didn't know if he'd heard her or not. He didn't nod or express even the slightest bit of awareness. But when she removed the tape and tugged on his arm, he struggled to his feet and allowed her to help him inside.

"This is a good sign," she told him as she guided him through the kitchen and into the living room. "Walking under your own steam like this. I'm thinking maybe you're not hurt so badly after all."

He said nothing.

Claudia maneuvered him into the bedroom and, against her better judgment, unwrapped the tape around his wrists so that she could help him out of his wet clothing. She did the latter in almost complete darkness, not because she was a prude or anything, but because she respected his privacy.

"If you turn out to be a killer, all bets are off," she

warned as she tugged off his jacket. He didn't offer so much as a flicker of protest, even when she peeled away his soaked shirt.

"I'll, uh, let you take care of the rest."

He stripped without a word.

The first thing that struck Claudia about him—well, maybe the second—was his demeanor. Perhaps because he was barely conscious, but he seemed as docile as a child. He shrugged out of his drenched clothing without comment or protest, then climbed into bed and allowed her to re-tape his wrists and ankles. Curling himself into a ball, he drifted off.

The electricity couldn't have been off that long, but it was already cold inside the cabin. Grabbing extra blankets from the closet, Claudia piled them on the bed, then stood for a moment gazing down at him.

Angling the flashlight beam over his face, she told herself she was checking for injuries, but truth be told, she wanted to get a better look at him. Carefully, she took stock: Dark hair, high cheekbones, a firm jaw and chin. Full lips.

Very full lips.

He had what she and her high-school girlfriends used to call a kissable mouth. Her first crush had had a kissable mouth.

So did this guy. This naked stranger in her bed.

Naked. Stranger. In her bed.

If she were the swooning type, she might feel a little

lightheaded at her current situation, but Claudia was no shrinking violet. She had a healthy respect for the human body and her own sexuality, but this little scenario pushed even her boundaries.

She reminded herself she was almost like a doctor here, and he, a patient in her care. She needed to make sure he wasn't seriously injured.

Or packing a concealed weapon somewhere.

Speaking of which…

She turned and scooped up his dripping clothes and quickly searched through all the pockets. No ID, no money, no car keys. Nothing. So he wasn't just an unlucky motorist then.

Unless, of course, he'd lost both his wallet and keys. Possible but not very likely.

"So who are you?" she murmured as she turned back to the bed.

"Cold…"

As she drew the down comforter up to his chin and tucked the spare blankets around him, her knuckles brushed against his cheek.

He stirred in his sleep. "Find her."

"Find who?"

"Danger."

Claudia swallowed. "Who's in danger?"

Silence.

She put her hand on his shoulder and gently shook him. "Hey! Who were you looking for out there? Who's in danger?" When he still didn't answer, she said in frustration, "Who the hell are you? And what am I supposed to do with you?"

"…kill me…" he whispered.

"What?"

He sighed in his sleep and was silent.

Chapter Four

Claudia left the bedroom door open so that she could hear him if he roused. Then she lit some candles, started a fire and after changing out of her wet clothes into some sweats, headed into the kitchen to put on the teakettle.

Ah, the luxury of a gas stove, she thought. At least the power outage wouldn't deprive her of a hot drink. Nothing like a nice cup of chamomile tea to warm chilled bones and relax taut nerves while waiting for the electricity to come back on.

The chamomile tea addiction was a by-product of her migration to the Black Hills. Back in Chicago, Claudia had preferred black coffee—gallons of it—to keep her alert during her long, tedious hours in the lab. Now she just needed to stay calm.

Her job as Dr. Lasher's research assistant had been to painstakingly analyze the mountains of number graphs spit out daily by strategically placed REGs—Random Event Generators. It had been Dr. Lasher's contention that each REG, which resembled a jetliner's black box, held within it the power to change the world by predicting natural and manmade catastrophes before they happened. And his theory had seemingly been validated when just four short hours before the planes hit the World Trade towers on 9/11, unusual spikes had been observed in the number sequences generated by REGs placed all over the world. Anomalies had also occurred hours before the Asian Tsunami had struck.

Of course, it was one thing to predict a catastrophic event using fluctuations in the number sequences, quite another to determine when and where it would occur and how to stop it. To that end, Dr. Lasher had eventually teamed up with a mysterious colleague who had supplied him with a test subject exhibiting signs of extraordinary precognitive abilities. Their goal was to create a "psychic" machine that interfaced a human pre-cog with the REG in order to better pinpoint pending global disasters.

But Dr. Lasher had come to regret that collaboration, once his suspicions panned out about his colleague. Turned out, he was involved with a covert multinational organization with nefarious plans for the project.

After his discovery, Dr. Lasher became tense and withdrawn, and when Claudia pressed him for more details, he'd mumble inane warnings that made little sense. But in combination with some unusual glitches in the REG graphs, his vague foreshadowing troubled her. She began to wonder if the disturbances in the number sequences were, in fact, indirect communications from the pre-cog. Maybe he was trying to warn her, too.

And then Dr. Lasher had been murdered, and that brief glimpse of the killer's face had told Claudia everything she needed to know. If she stayed in Chicago, she would be next. The police couldn't protect her. No one could.

Leaving the city by cover of darkness, she'd driven north by northwest for no particular reason that she could explain. The strange compulsion had eventually led her to Rapid City where she'd rented her little hideaway in the woods and begun a whole new life.

With her research days behind her, Claudia now made a modest living as a website designer, a career that perfectly suited someone who needed to fly underneath the radar. She called her business North by Northwest Designs, and even her most trusted clients were not privy to her real name.

She'd taken other precautions as well, and up until tonight, she'd almost begun to believe that she was safe there.

Now she wasn't so sure. The stranger's presence made her uneasy in a way she hadn't been for a long, long time.

There was something about him that just didn't seem right. The way he'd appeared so suddenly in front of her car…that unnatural glow in his eyes…

Her thoughts scattered as the high-pitched whistle of

the kettle caused her to jump. Then she let out a shaky laugh as she hurried into the kitchen. Obviously, she needed her chamomile tea fix in the worst way.

Carrying the steaming brew into the living room, she grabbed her laptop and settled in before the fire. Luckily, her battery was fully charged and she also had a spare. Since she had no intention of closing her eyes while a strange man was in her bed, she might as well get a little work done. Come morning, when the road had been cleared, she'd take him into town, drop him at the hospital or the police station and wash her hands of the whole nerve-wracking affair.

As she scrolled through her stored images, searching for the right color combination for a collage header, she heard a sound from the bedroom. The incoherent mumble set Claudia's blood tingling.

Who was he talking to?

Setting the laptop aside, she rose and grabbed the flashlight and pistol, then eased up to the door. Her gaze tracked the light beam from his form on the bed to every corner of the room. He was alone.

Just to be on the safe side, she crossed to the window and checked the lock.

The delirious rambling started up again, and as Claudia walked slowly toward the bed, she experienced an inexplicable feeling of familiarity. Not déjà vu exactly, but something close to it. Something that deepened the chill in her bones and caused her pulse to race. What on earth was going on here?

She was just a little jittery, she told herself. And rightfully so. Having a stranger in the house was enough to unsettle anyone, but given her particular circumstances, she had every right to be on edge.

And if her unease manifested itself in some peculiar sensations, well…that was probably to be expected. She was only human. A human with a terrifying past and a vivid imagination.

Taking a deep breath to steady herself, Claudia inched up to the bed. The stranger's eyes were shut, but she could see the rapid movement beneath the lids as he continued to mutter. She couldn't make out anything he said, and after a few moments, she adjusted the cover and moved away.

But at the door, she paused to glance back. A little shiver touched her spine, like the sweep of a moth, and she found herself glancing around the chilled room yet again. No one was there. She and the stranger were alone. And yet it was almost as if she could feel another presence, a quietly persistent manifestation that moved and faded with the shadows.

Help him.

"What?" Her gaze shot to the stranger but he hadn't moved, and she was pretty sure he hadn't spoken. No one had. And yet for a fleeting moment, the voice inside Claudia's head was all too real.

Help him.

A crawling sense of dread tightened her throat. "Who are you?" she whispered.

Help him. Please.

Almost against her will, her gaze went back to the bed. "It's okay," she said softly. "You're safe here."

The mumbling stopped. The voice inside her head faded, and the cabin in the aftermath was so hushed, Claudia could hear the soft expulsion of the stranger's breath.

Then his voice rose and she started.

"Where are you? *Where are you?*" he asked desperately.

Apprehension prickled the back of her neck. "I'm right here."

"Why can't I see you?"

"I'm right here," she soothed, even though her heart pounded like a racehorse's hooves against her chest. She swallowed. "Everything's fine."

"She's not there anymore," he said in despair.

"Who's not?"

"She's gone. I can't find her."

"Find who?"

"...danger..."

"Who's in danger?"

"The girl inside my head," he murmured, and for the first time that night, Claudia had a feeling he was speaking directly to her.

The girl inside my head.

God help me, she thought as she backed away from the door. She really had brought a lunatic into her home.

A lunatic with an uncanny ability of making her care.

Chapter Five

It took a long time and a lot of patience, but he finally managed to rip off the tape around his wrists with his teeth, then freed his ankles and sat up in bed. Traces of the dream still swirled inside his head, and he pressed his fingers to his temples to sharpen the focus.

If he could just see those images a little more clearly, he might be able to make sense of them. He might actually be able to save her.

Because the one thing that was deadly apparent to him was the encroaching danger. They were coming. He didn't know when or how, but they were coming. And they would kill her unless he could find a way to stop them.

The throbbing at his temples grew stronger, and he fell back against the pillow, wanting for a moment to draw the covers up over his head and disappear once again into his dreams.

But the sound of her voice had lulled him from sleep and now he had plans to make, traps to set.

Destiny was speeding toward him faster than a freight train, and he had no way to stop it. The only thing he could do was change it.

But first he had to convince the woman she was in grave danger. And that he wasn't crazy.

For the latter, he really wished he had his clothes.

Chapter Six

Claudia stood at the window for the longest time. The storm had moved off to the east. The rain had dwindled to a drizzle and the lighting was a mere flicker on the horizon. Now that the thunder had faded, the night was almost unbearably still.

In spite of the roaring fire, she felt a terrible chill. The cold was pervasive. It seeped in under the doors and around the window panes and settled over the room like a shroud.

And with the cold came a dark dread.

Was someone out there?

Shuddering, she searched the darkness. Was she being watched at that very moment?

She tried to shake off her growing anxiety, told herself she was letting her imagination and her current predicament get the better of her, but the longer she peered into the darkness, the more convinced she became that someone was staring back at her.

It's okay. The doors and windows are locked, and I'm armed and ready. No one can get in.

But what if the danger was already inside the house with her?

Now you are letting your imagination run away with you.

Was she really, though? She'd brought a stranger into her home, and that was never a good idea, no matter the circumstances.

Earlier, it had seemed as if she'd had no choice, but now Claudia had to wonder. Maybe she should have left him where she'd found him. All his mumbling about danger…that couldn't be coming from a good place.

Who dashes out into the middle of an isolated road on a cold, rainy night?

Someone on the run, that was who.

An escaped convict, maybe, or someone fleeing from the scene of a fresh crime.

And she had brought him into her home.

Help him.

Where had that plea come from earlier? Had she manufactured that voice inside her head? Was it a manifestation of her guilt for having come so close to running him down?

Help him? Hadn't she done just that by setting her own safety aside and letting him into her house? What more could she do for him?

This was so not good. For two whole years, she'd been so careful, painstakingly charting every course, meticulously planning every move and now in the space of a heartbeat, she'd put everything on the line.

Wrapping her arms around her middle, she started to turn away from the window, but in the flash of distant lightning, she saw something at the edge of the woods. A silhouette that looked about the height and size of a large man.

With a sharp sense of shock, Claudia peeled her eyes to the spot, stomach muscles contracting, nerve endings tingling with sick fear. But in another flicker of lightning, she saw that it was only a tree.

She really was letting the night get the better of her, so much so that a shifting log had the effect of a shotgun blast in the silent room. Rattled by her reaction, she walked back over to the fireplace and forced herself to calmly stoke the flames as she gave herself a little pep talk.

All she had to do was stay calm and in control. Morning would come soon. She would drive the stranger into town and she'd never see him again. Her life would settle back into the same routine, and that would be that.

The same routine.

For a moment, loneliness edged away the cold and the fear, and Claudia was given a glimpse of how easy it would be to throw caution to the wind for a fleeting companionship. She was only twenty-four, much too young to be living the sterile existence of a hermit. She craved friends, nightlife, someone special to keep her warm and safe on cold, wet nights.

The solitude of the woods and the isolation of the cabin could sometimes wear her down to the point of risking everything for a single phone call to an old friend. Then she would remember what had been done to Dr. Lasher, and her resolve would be bolstered all over again.

Facing death was one thing, torture quite another.

She warmed her hands over the flames, then picked up her cup. The tea had already cooled, so she drifted back into the kitchen to put the kettle on again. Waiting for the water to boil, she returned to the window, anxious and vigilant.

It wasn't just her imagination and it wasn't just the strange situation she found herself in. Something wasn't right. She could feel it. The unpleasant sensation that nested in the hollow of her chest seemed to grow and tighten with each breath she drew.

So engrossed was she in trying to analyze her trepidation that she didn't hear the creak of the bed or the soft footfalls that stopped at the open doorway. She never heard a thing, but something alerted her to his presence. A premonition or some imperceptible shift in the air currents. Or that voice in her head maybe. Something…

She turned and there he stood.

As naked as the day he was born.

The candles and fire had burned down so that a soft, flickering glow illuminated the room. He was mostly in shadows, but nothing was left to Claudia's imagination. She caught her breath at the sheer symmetry of his form. He was all lean muscle and intriguing angles.

As their gazes met across the murky room, she felt something fiery shoot through her midsection, like a crumbling meteorite streaking its way toward earth. The collision was inevitable, and yet she couldn't look away. For a moment, she had the crazy urge to rush toward it with arms wide open.

She even took a step toward him and then thankfully good sense prevailed. "Is something wrong?" she asked on a shaky breath.

He said nothing.

She frowned at his unblinking stare. "Are you okay?"

A longer silence.

He was starting to make her even more nervous. "I know you can speak," she said. "I heard you talk in your sleep."

And then it hit her that he had freed himself. Terror curled in her stomach as she realized just how vulnerable she now was.

Don't panic. Keep a cool head.

What she needed to do was arm herself as quickly and unobtrusively as she could. The gun was on her desk, just to the left of the front door. She needed to somehow get to it without setting off any alarms.

"The weapon won't help you," he said.

Claudia froze. "What?"

"You're going to die," he said ominously. "And there will be nothing you can do to stop it."

Chapter Seven

Claudia lunged for the gun, grasped the grip in both hands and whirled to face him. "Don't move! I'll shoot. That I promise you."

He hadn't set foot outside the bedroom doorway, and now he gazed at her in bewilderment. "I'm not here to hurt you. I came to save you."

"Save me?"

Dear God, could that be true? Had someone really sent him here to protect her?

But who? Not even her closest friends knew where she'd run off to or why. She hadn't even clued in the police.

And why now, after two years of being on her own?

It didn't make sense. Nothing about this whole crazy situation made any sense, especially her reaction to him. She was afraid and fascinated all at the same time.

And against her better judgment, she felt a welling hope nudge away her suspicion. But only for a moment.

Then her defenses came back up, and she steeled her spine and tightened her grip on the revolver.

Be careful here. Remember your motto: trust no one.

Thankfully, her good sense and natural skepticism came rushing back full force. Maybe he was just trying to catch her off guard. Why he hadn't attacked her when her back was to him, she had no idea. Obviously, his agenda included more than just murder.

You're going to die and there will be nothing you can do to stop it.

Her chin shot up. *We'll just see about that.*

She wouldn't go quietly. That was for damn sure.

Still, she prayed it wouldn't come to that. But if he meant her harm, the gun was her best defense. She just hoped he couldn't see how badly her hands trembled. She was shaking so hard she didn't dare put a finger on the trigger. *Never put a finger on the trigger unless you're prepared to shoot.* She wasn't. Not until he made the first move. Then she would blast away. Not without regret, but certainly without hesitation.

She clutched the grip. "Who are you?"

"My name is…Jack Maddox."

The way he paused before he revealed his name reinforced her suspicions. He'd probably pulled that name out of thin air. "Are you sure about that?"

"Yes."

"Who sent you here?"

"…sent me?" He touched fingertips to his temples and pressed. "I…don't know."

"What do you mean, you don't know?"

"I don't...know."

Her eyes narrowed. "How did you find me?"

"I don't know."

This was going nowhere fast.

Claudia glared at him. "What were you doing out there on the road all alone tonight?"

"I don't know."

"Where did you come from?"

"I don't know."

"Were you in some sort of accident?" *Well, duh.* Although, whether she'd actually hit him or not was still up for debate.

"I don't know."

"How can you not know these things?" she asked in frustration.

His dark gaze held hers for the longest moment. "I've been...erased."

A hair-prickling draft lifted the hair at the back of Claudia's neck, as if a ghost had just slipped past her. She resisted the urge to glance over her shoulder. "Erased? What are you talking about?"

"I don't...remember." The fingertips pressed more deeply into his temples. He squeezed his eyes closed and swayed for a moment as if his knees were about to buckle. Then his lids snapped open and he caught her in the most penetrating gaze she'd ever endured. Suddenly, it was Claudia who felt a little weak in the knees.

She tried to suppress a shiver as that dark gaze held hers. "Are you saying you have amnesia?"

"Amnesia? Yes…I have amnesia." His hands dropped to his sides. Claudia tried not to follow the motion.

The way he said amnesia without any inflection seemed to suggest he was merely repeating a word he didn't quite comprehend. But how could he not know the meaning of amnesia? He obviously spoke English and he didn't strike Claudia as illiterate. Something about him just didn't compute, though, and the conversation went beyond peculiar. It was downright disturbing.

"I need you to believe me," he said.

And I need you to get your crazy ass out of my house.

Maybe it was only the flicker of candlelight, but somehow he seemed bathed in an ethereal blush. There was just something so truly weird about him. About all of this.

And he was just so…naked.

"What do you need me to believe?" she demanded.

"The danger…"

"Oh, I'm very interested in hearing all about this danger you keep talking about. But first could you…do something about that?" She waved the gun over his naked form. Killer or not, the play of shadow and light on all those lean muscles was very distracting. "Throw a blanket around yourself or something."

He vanished back into the bedroom to comply, and Claudia tried to compose herself before he reappeared a moment later in the doorway.

"That's better," she said. "As soon as the power comes back on, we can dry your clothes." If she didn't kick him out in the cold first.

"Thank you."

Such sincerity. Such humble gratitude. He wasn't making this easy for her. "What did you mean earlier when you said I was going to die and there would be nothing I could do to stop it?"

"It's true," he said. "You won't be able to stop it… but I can."

"How?"

"By changing your destiny."

"Well, that's mighty big of you." *Crazy as a loon,* Claudia thought.

"I came here to save you."

"So you keep saying. Just who are you saving me from?"

"Those who wish to kill you."

"How do you know—" She caught herself and paused with another shiver. "What makes you think someone wants to kill me?"

He gave her a strange, probing look.

Then his gaze shifted to the kitchen a split second before the teakettle began to whistle.

Before the teakettle whistled.

Now it was Claudia who gave him a hard stare as she hurried into the kitchen to turn off the burner.

She placed the gun on the counter within easy reach and was just debating on whether to offer him tea—

which would hopefully keep him calm—when he asked from across the room, "What is chamomile?"

Slowly, she turned to face him. "Why did you ask that?"

Then out of the corner of her eye, she spotted the container of teabags by the stove and realized he must have read the side of the tin. Whatever else might be wrong with him, he obviously had excellent eyesight and hearing.

"You've never had chamomile tea?" When he didn't answer, she muttered, "I guess you wouldn't remember if you've been erased."

Erased.

Good heavens.

"Chamomile is a member of the daisy family," she said, striving for a conversational tone. The last thing she wanted to do was inadvertently set him off. There was a good possibility that instead of coming here to murder her, he could be just some troubled soul who'd stumbled into the middle of the road at an inopportune time. In which case, the best thing to do was try and keep him calm. "The tea is an acquired taste, but it's wonderfully relaxing. Would you like a cup?"

She could do with a bit of stress relief herself, Claudia thought.

When he started toward her, she said quickly, "No, no, that's okay. Just stay there. I'll bring it to you."

She got down a second cup and poured hot water over the teabag. When it had properly steeped, she mixed in a little lemon and honey, then grabbed the gun and carried the drink into the living room where she placed it on a table in front of the fire.

Returning to the kitchen, she fixed herself a fresh cup. By the time she came back into the living room, he'd settled himself on the floor before the fire.

"Make yourself at home," she murmured.

He picked up the cup and took a tentative sip of the tea. "Tastes like flowers."

"As I said, it's an acquired taste."

He drank some more. "It's hot. Feels good."

"You must have gotten a chill out there in the rain. It's pretty cold tonight and your clothes were soaking wet."

That was another thing about him that puzzled Claudia. His shirt, pants and lightweight jacket were hardly suitable for November weather in the Black Hills. Not to mention his canvas shoes, which were drenched all the way through. It was a wonder he didn't have frostbite.

But maybe the inappropriate clothing wasn't so strange after all. Before the storm, they'd been enjoying a warm spell in the area. The daytime temperatures had been so mild that Claudia had even been able to continue her morning hikes to enhance her cardio workout.

With the storm, the thermometer had dropped to a more seasonable chill, reminding her that soon enough the snows would come. She would be sequestered in the cabin for long days at a time, sometimes with no phone or power. Not a single, solitary soul to keep her company.

She shuddered in dread.

Better lonely than dead, she reminded herself.

But back to the stranger…

Perching on the arm of a chair, she rested the revolver on her thigh as she sipped her tea and watched him. He had the blanket wrapped around him, and the way he gulped the hot drink made him seem young and kind of endearing.

But in the glow of the fire, Claudia could see the muscle definition in his bare arms and shoulders. He was strong and probably anything but vulnerable. If she let down her guard for even a second, he could easily overpower her.

"Let's talk about this memory loss of yours." She set the teacup aside, but kept the gun on her thigh.

He put down his tea and gazed up at her, looking very mysterious and downright ethereal with the light flickering over his features. His dark hair was cropped short and Claudia had the sudden notion that if he wasn't an escaped mental patient, he might be in the military or law enforcement. That could explain how he'd found her. Maybe someone was finally looking into the group responsible for Dr. Lasher's murder. Maybe he had been sent to protect her.

Then again, for all she knew, he could have been sent by the people who wanted her dead. She couldn't lose sight of the danger he potentially posed just because he had nice eyes and kept insisting that he'd come there to save her.

"What's the last thing you remember?" she asked.

He blinked. "The woods. The road. You."

"In other words, you don't remember anything before tonight?"

He sighed and seemed to settle more deeply into the blanket. "I don't want to remember."

"Why not?"

He closed his eyes and shuddered. "…Pain…"

"You remember pain? Then maybe you were in some sort of accident. A car wreck maybe." It was possible he'd been so dazed and confused, he'd wandered miles from the scene of the crash and then stumbled into the path of her oncoming vehicle.

"The needles hurt," he said.

Something in his voice—a faint note of fear, nothing more—brought the image of a caged animal to Claudia's mind. For a moment, she forgot about the possible threat he brought with him. She even forgot to breathe.

He turned to stare into the flames. "I don't like memories."

Claudia's heart beat so hard against her chest, she could hear the echo in her ears.

I don't like memories.

What on earth had happened to him?

And why did she have an irresistible urge to kneel beside him on the floor and wrap her arms around him?

Why, suddenly, did she want to save *him?*

This made no sense. She could feel compassion without chucking her common sense. He was still a stranger and she still had to protect herself.

And as for the needles…an escapee from a psychiatric ward might have such memories, mightn't he?

She bit her lip. "I can understand why you may not like memories," she said softly. "But if we're going to figure out why you're here and why you think I need saving, then we need to know if there's anything else you can tell me."

He stared into the fire for a long time, and then his gaze lifted. "*Coronet Blue.*"

"I'm sorry?"

"That's what I remember," he said. "*Coronet Blue.*"

And then, quite unexpectedly, he smiled.

Chapter Eight

Claudia decided the best thing to do was call it a night and figure things out in the morning. Her interrogation had accomplished nothing. If the man really did have amnesia, he needed to be under a doctor's care. There wasn't anything she could do for him and her questions might just upset him.

Though he didn't seem upset at the moment. Not with that smile he'd just flashed. It was a little sly, a little knowing, as if he were enjoying a private joke. At her expense.

Claudia didn't care for that.

Which was yet another reason why she had no intention of closing her eyes while he was in her house. She would not rest easy until Jack Maddox—if that was his real name—was out of her life for good.

"I think—"

Before she had a chance to finish her thought, he said, "I'll stay out here. If that's permitted."

Permitted?

The way he spoke was yet another intriguing piece of the puzzle, as was his ability to anticipate the direction of her thoughts. She'd been on the verge of suggesting that he take the bedroom, but once again he'd interpreted her intention before she had a chance to say anything. His insight was uncanny. Disturbingly so.

"Maybe you should take the bed," she said. "You need your rest."

"Why? I'm not hurt or sick."

Well, except for that amnesia thing.

But come to think of it, the bedroom door did have a lock on the inside, so maybe that arrangement was for the best, Claudia decided.

"If that's the way you want it. Hopefully, by morning you'll have remembered something else." As she spoke, she moved around the room, gathering up the flashlight, her handbag with her cell phone and wallet inside, her laptop and, of course, the gun. The only thing left of any real value was her desktop computer, and somehow she didn't see him grabbing that up and making a run with it through the rain.

His dark gaze tracked her every move. When she had everything she needed, he held out his hands. "Do you want to bind them again?"

She gave it serious consideration, but obviously it hadn't done much good the first time.

"You don't need to worry," he said solemnly. "I won't let anyone hurt you."

He said it so convincingly, she almost believed him.

And she had to ask herself, *Now who's the lunatic?*

At the bedroom door, she glanced back. He was sitting exactly where she'd left him before the fire, but rather than staring into the flames, he was still looking at her. His intense focus made her tremble, although she wanted to believe it was just the cold.

"See you in the morning," she said.

"Good night…"

"Claudia." Too late, she realized that she probably shouldn't have told him her name, but if he worked for the men who wanted her dead—or even for the government—her identity was obviously no secret.

Back in Chicago, she'd gone by C.J. Her given name was Claudia Janelle, but she'd never used it until she moved here. Even after all this time, she still wasn't used to it.

"It doesn't suit you," he said.

She frowned. "Why not?"

"It's an old name."

"I wouldn't mention that to Claudia Schiffer if you happen to run into her."

"I won't," he said solemnly.

She shook her head at his apparent oblivion to her pop-culture reference. "Whatever. The name suits me fine. I have an old soul."

With that, she opened the bedroom door and went inside. Locking herself in, she leaned against the door, shivering in the cold.

This was so not how she'd planned to spend the

night. Actually, her nights took very little planning because they were all the same. Dinner alone by the fire or, in warm weather, on the deck. Then she would listen to some music or watch a little television. Surf the 'Net, read a book, work into the wee hours. Anything to eat up all those long, lonely hours.

If nothing else, tonight had been a break from the relentless tedium her young life had become.

Placing the gun and laptop on the nightstand and her handbag on the floor, she used the flashlight to locate spare linens in the closet. Then getting the bed all set up the way she wanted, she cocooned herself in the cover.

With the flashlight off, the room was pitch black. The night seemed to close in on her, and Claudia lay there for the longest time, staring into the darkness and willing her eyes to remain open, no matter how heavy her lids became.

Chapter Nine

The click of the lock sent a deep shudder through Jack. He knew that sound, and a claustrophobic dread descended over him as he threw off the cover and got to his feet.

He went first to the front door to make sure he wasn't locked in. When he drew it back, a burst of cold, wet air rushed over him, and he stood for a moment, staring out into the dark and listening to the sounds of the receding storm.

Satisfied there was no imminent threat, he closed the door and went to each window, assuring himself that there were no bars caging him in. He was still free.

And he had found her. The girl inside his head.

She was still in grave danger, but not tonight. He was with her now and he would do everything in his considerable power to keep her safe.

If she would let him.

That was the tricky part. She didn't trust him and he couldn't blame her for that. He was nothing to her, and there was very little he could tell her that would reassure her of his intent. But somehow he'd have to convince her just the same. He would have to make her believe him because her life—and his—depended on it.

After a bit of foraging in the kitchen, he sat down at the table with an apple and a can of nuts he'd found in the pantry. He ate fast and after his appetite was somewhat sated, he prowled some more.

It was odd that he could remember almost nothing of his past except for his name, and yet there were objects in Claudia's house that he easily recognized. The computer, for instance. He knew something about that. And the remote control to the television set. He knew even more about that.

Settling himself on the sofa, he tried to click on the TV, but the power was still out. Too bad.

Because what he wanted to do more than anything at that moment was to watch his favorite episode of *Starsky and Hutch.*

Chapter Ten

Claudia's eyes flew open. She heard voices coming from the other room.

Someone was in the house!

Someone besides Jack Maddox.

He must have let them in. And maybe they were out there right now conspiring on how to kill her. Or which one of them would get to do it!

Easing her legs over the side of the bed, she rose and grabbed her gun from the nightstand. Tiptoeing across the darkened room to the door, she checked the lock. It was still secure, but it wouldn't take much to kick it open.

She pressed her ear to the wood and listened. The voices were so low she couldn't make out any of the conversation, or even how many were out there. But she was almost certain she could hear a female voice.

And laughter. Canned laughter.

Oh, for heaven's sakes...

He was watching television. The power must have come back on while she'd been sleeping.

Claudia opened the door a crack and peered out. He'd moved from the floor up to the couch where he sat cross-legged with the blanket around him as he watched the flickering screen. He was so engrossed in whatever he had on he didn't even notice when Claudia pulled the door open and stepped out.

Slipping the revolver into the pocket of her sweater, she walked over to the couch. "What are you watching?"

He didn't appear to hear her at first.

She took a peek at the screen. "Kind of late for *The Brady Bunch,* isn't it?"

He turned slowly and looked up at her with wide, innocent eyes. They were blue, she realized with a start. Earlier, the irises had appeared so dark, she'd thought them black, but no. His eyes were most definitely a deep, riveting blue.

"I'm sorry. Did I disturb you?" he asked politely.

The apology was so earnest, Claudia found herself rushing to reassure him. "No, it's fine. After everything you've been through, I just figured you needed to rest."

His gaze had already returned to the screen.

"You like TV, huh?"

"I've never seen this show before," he said.

"You've got to be kidding," she said in astonishment. "It's always on rerun somewhere. And all the episodes are pretty much the same so you don't have to be clairvoyant to figure out what happens." She bent to pick up the empty teacup from the end table. "Marsha will come out smelling like a rose and Jan will somehow get the shaft."

"I'm not clairvoyant," he said.

"It was just a figure of speech. I didn't mean to imply—"

"I'm a pre-cog."

The teacup slipped from her fingers. The porcelain would have shattered against the hardwood floor if his hand hadn't already shot out to catch it. Almost as if he'd known beforehand she would drop it...

Her gaze lifted. "What did you say?"

"I'm a pre-cog. It means I have the ability to—"

"I know what it means," Claudia said hoarsely.

Suddenly, her head was full of flashing images. The way he'd anticipated her move toward the gun. The way he'd heard the teakettle before it whistled. The way he'd asked her about chamomile when she'd been on the verge of offering him some.

And now the way his hand had sprung out to catch the cup before she dropped it.

Anyone else would have looked for a more logical explanation. Fast reflexes. Twenty-twenty vision and keen hearing. An uncanny ability to read people. But Claudia knew from her work with Dr. Lasher that for some people, the ability to foretell future events was as real as their five senses.

What she didn't understand was how someone with this gift had ended up in her remote cabin. This couldn't be a coincidence. Someone had sent him.

She whirled toward the front door. Her first instinct was to make a run for it, but he was already there, blocking her way and she froze.

He'd moved so quickly, the blanket had been left behind on the couch. He stood before her in all his naked glory. Any other time, Claudia might have appreciated the view, but suddenly she was more frightened than she'd been in a long, long time.

"Who are you?" she demanded.

"I've told you my name." He took a step toward her.

She pulled the gun from her pocket and drew a bead. "Don't come any closer."

"I'm not going to hurt you. I came here to save you."

"Stop saying that! I don't believe a word out of your mouth. Someone sent you here. This can't be a coincidence. You...me...*here* in the middle of nowhere? Someone planned this."

"I don't understand."

"I know what a pre-cog is," she said desperately. "I've studied precognitive abilities. I may be the only person in this whole area, in the whole damn *state* that wouldn't blink an eye at your claim. And of all the cars on all the roads on any given night, you pick my car on this night to run out in front of. *Why?*"

"I have to save you."

"I said stop it! Just tell me the truth! Why are you here?"

"I came to—"

"Don't come any closer!" she warned when he took

another step toward her. "I swear to God, I'll put a bullet right through your chest."

"Claudia...please, listen to me..."

The persuasive quality of his voice shook her. It seemed hypnotic, almost vampiric in its ability to seduce.

The light from the television screen flickered over his naked body, and the dichotomy of light and shadow threatened to mesmerize her yet again.

"I won't hurt you," he repeated softly. "You have to believe me."

And God help her, she wanted to. She really did.

She drew a shuddering breath. "Just keep your distance."

"I can't do that. You have to know something."

"I'm warning you...*stay where you are*..."

But he moved toward her until he was standing before her. She was a tall woman, but he seemed to tower over her, and her knees suddenly weakened. She had the strongest compulsion to steady herself by placing her hands on his bare chest.

She refrained, even managed to back up a step and keep the gun between them.

He didn't follow her, but instead lifted a hand to touch her cheek. "You know me," he murmured.

"I've never set eyes on you before tonight!"

His fingertips slid down her cheek. "You know me."

"*No.*" But the gun dropped to her side as her other hand came up to close over his. Her whole body tingled at the contact, and the throb of her heart became a painful staccato against the wall of her chest. For the longest time, she stood with her eyes closed, drinking him in.

She did know him. There was something so thrillingly familiar about the touch of his hand, the sound of his voice. The way he looked at her. Claudia had never seen him before tonight, but somehow, she did know him.

She opened her mouth, whether to confirm or deny his assertion, she wasn't quite certain. But just then, the front door flew open and she screamed.

Instantly, he leaped in front of her, putting himself between her and the icy wind that swept through the cabin.

And in that moment, Claudia had no doubt that if a gunman had stood in the doorway, Jack Maddox would have taken a bullet for her.

THANKFULLY, THERE WAS NO gunman on the front porch.

As it turned out, there was nothing at all but the wind. The lock must not have been fully engaged and a strong gust had whipped it open, although Claudia was usually very careful about making sure the premises were secured at all times. Still, she wasn't infallible.

And even though there had been no real threat, she couldn't discount Jack's actions. He'd been willing to put himself on the line for her, and now she couldn't help but look at him in a different light.

Of course, if he really did have precognitive abilities, it was possible he'd foreseen the outcome. He could have known before the door blew open that no one was out there. But Claudia didn't think that was the case. His instincts had been real enough and so had his intentions.

Besides, she knew from her work with Dr. Lasher that even the most gifted pre-cog wasn't omniscient. He couldn't know everything that was about to happen at every minute of the day. Most of the time, it took a great deal of focus and concentration. And right now, his focus seemed to be trained on her.

While he closed and locked the front door, Claudia walked to the window, her gaze sweeping over the darkened landscape. Her earlier uneasiness had abated somewhat, and now she felt the heavy cloak of exhaustion descend over her. If she was to have the physical and mental fortitude to deal with whatever the morning brought, she needed to get some rest.

Oddly, where only a short time ago she'd been determined to remain awake with a stranger in the house, she could only think now of sleep.

"It's okay," he said, his eyes fastened on hers. "I'm here. You'll be safe."

The amount of comfort that statement gave her was something Claudia knew she needed to worry about, but didn't.

What a strange, strange night, she thought as she left the room and climbed back into bed.

Chapter Eleven

A few hours later, Claudia opened her eyes to a gloomy morning. Getting out of bed, she padded over to the window to glance out. The rain had moved on during the night, but the sky was still a dismal gray and high up in the hills, patches of fog hovered over the treetops.

The house was warm now, but she still couldn't help shivering when she thought of last night's events. She'd brought a stranger into her house who claimed to have precognitive abilities. Who claimed to have turned up in front of her vehicle because he wanted to save her.

From those who wish to kill you.

Even if Claudia could believe any of that—and a part of her really wanted to—how had he known where to find her? Had his vision of her impending doom been that vivid? How was it that he could foretell the future of someone he'd never even met?

She thought of the way he'd touched her face and her hand crept to her cheek. *You know me.*

Yes, she thought. *At that moment, I did know him, but*

how is that even possible when I never set eyes on him before last night?

There was an explanation for their strange connection, but Claudia wasn't so certain she wanted to go there.

One theory regarding precognition suggested that time moved both forward and backward, in which case the predicting of future events was actually the recollection of things that had already taken place. Certain gifted people had the ability to tap into these collective memories, thus allowing them to see things before they happened in the present.

In such a scenario, everything that had happened last night…had happened before. That would explain why Jack Maddox seemed so familiar to her.

Claudia didn't necessarily buy into that premise, but no matter how he came by the ability, she didn't see how any of this could be random. Jack Maddox had shown up here for a reason, and she would do well to swallow everything he told her with a healthy dose of skepticism. He'd almost had her convinced last night that he was, in fact, her savior, but now in the cold light of day, she realized how foolish she would be to accept his word at face value.

Something was definitely going on. She hadn't figured it out yet, but whatever his motive, she had to believe she'd been better off before he came into her life and she would be better off still when he left. The last thing she wanted was to be pulled back into the nightmare she'd fled from in Chicago.

Unlocking the door, she peeked out and saw that he was still sleeping. He lay on the floor in front of the fireplace, facing the front door, and at the moment, he seemed dead to the world.

Some guardian, Claudia scoffed as she retreated back into the bedroom and snatched clean clothes from her closet. Then she headed for the bathroom where she locked herself in again and had a nice, long shower. By the time she finally came out, she expected to find him up and about, but he hadn't moved a muscle since she'd checked on him earlier.

Tiptoeing past him, she hurried out to the small laundry room and retrieved his clothes from the dryer, including the canvas shoes. Folding everything into a neat pile, she carried them into the house and carefully placed the stack on the floor beside him.

As she bent over him, she took a daylight appraisal. He still looked young, late twenties at the most, and in such deep repose, utterly devastating. What was it about him that tugged at her heart so?

He had several tiny round bruises on the right side of his neck. Some of them had faded to yellow, but one was still a fresh, prominent purple. Claudia leaned in to get a better look, but when he stirred and rolled onto his back, she scampered away like a frightened squirrel.

When he finally opened his eyes a few moments later and sat up, she was in the kitchen, nonchalantly making coffee. She noticed out of the corner of her eye that he didn't look around to get his bearings as one might do when waking up in a strange place. Instead, his gaze fastened like a laser on her.

Such an intense focus made her clumsy and she ended up spilling coffee grounds all over the counter. "Damn."

He started to get up, seemed to remember that he didn't have any clothes on and pulled the blanket around him.

"Your clothes are dry," she said as she nodded toward the stack on the floor. "If you want to get cleaned up, I left fresh towels and a spare toothbrush in the bathroom. Just help yourself."

"Thank you."

Claudia turned back to the coffeemaker as he got to his feet, but she couldn't help sneaking another quick peek from the corner of her eye.

Give the man some privacy, for goodness sakes!

Not that she could see much with that blanket wrapped around him anyway. And besides, it wasn't as if she hadn't already seen the whole package, so to speak. No wonder there was a strong sense of familiarity about him. Nothing about him had been left to her imagination.

That wasn't his fault, of course. She was the one who'd partially stripped off his wet clothing the night before.

Enough!

Just stop thinking about it, she chided herself. *All this excitement and drama over a naked man.* She really had been alone too long.

Her one-track mind was so annoying, especially

considering there were many more important things to focus on. Like who might have sent him and why. Like how quickly she could get him out of her house.

But…first things first. Food and coffee and then she'd kick him out.

BY THE TIME HE EMERGED from the bathroom, showered and dressed, Claudia had breakfast ready. "Hungry?"

A slight hesitation. "Yes."

"I didn't know what you'd want so I made a little of everything. Bacon and eggs, toast, coffee…"

"Thank you."

So unfailingly polite.

She nodded toward the small table by the window. "Have a seat. I'll bring you a plate."

"I can…serve myself," he said, and that curious pause made her wonder about him all over again.

Who are *you? Where did you come from and why are you here?*

And what am I going to do about you?

When she set a heaping plate in front of him, he waited until she was seated before he picked up his fork. He ate with a kind of studied restraint that suggested his first inclination was to devour the food before it could be taken away from him. At one point, he even curled an arm around his plate, as if guarding it from a hungry interloper, but then he seemed to catch himself and from that moment on, ate with impeccable manners.

Claudia tried to follow suit, but she couldn't seem to stop staring at him. Now that her initial fear had abated, she found him endlessly absorbing. Everything about him was just so curious.

And he really was gorgeous. Not that looks mattered all that much to her. Some of the friends and colleagues she'd admired most back in Chicago were quite ordinary in appearance, but Claudia had found them no less interesting or desirable. Intelligence and a strong sense of self worth had always been primary attractors for her, but she was only human, after all. And she'd been on her own for a very long time. She wondered how much her loneliness contributed to her current fascination with the stranger.

To be fair, though, the situation was truly bizarre. Neither her solitude nor her imagination had conjured up the intriguing enigma that called himself Jack Maddox.

"You never asked how it was that you came to be here," she said as she reached for her orange juice.

"You brought me here."

"Yes, but don't you want to know why?"

He stopped eating and glanced up.

When their eyes met, she quickly glanced away. "Do you remember what happened out there on the road?"

He seemed to reflect on the question for a moment. "I saw your headlights."

"Yes, and then you somehow ended up in the middle of the road right in front of my car." She took a sip of the juice. "I may have even hit you."

"You didn't hit me."

"Then why did you collapse in front of my vehicle? You were pretty out of it when I brought you here."

"I—"

He didn't finish his thought and Claudia glanced over with a prompt, "Yes?"

Something in his eyes sent a shockwave through her nervous system. For a split second, he looked as frightened and panicked as a deer trapped in a headlight. Then he caught himself and shook it off.

But Claudia had seen that look of abject horror on his face. She'd witnessed something in his eyes that she was almost certain he'd never meant to reveal.

My God, she thought on a breath. What had been done to him?

Images of Dr. Lasher's mutilated body floated up through the dark layers of her memory, and she had to swallow hard to keep from revealing her own inner terror.

"Did...someone hurt you?" she asked tentatively.

He glanced down at his plate. "I'm not hurt."

That didn't answer the question. "But you are," she insisted. "You have amnesia. Even if my car didn't hit you, it's possible you struck your head when you fell. You need to see a doctor."

"No doctor!" He jumped to his feet so quickly, the chair toppled over with a crash.

His vehemence startled Claudia. It was the first time he'd raised his voice and fear rocketed through her veins. His outburst was a graphic reminder that she could be dealing with someone whose mental state was precarious at best. Extreme caution was definitely warranted.

She was suddenly very glad for the comforting weight of the revolver in her sweater pocket. Her fingers itched to close around the grip, but she remained still as she stared up at him.

Then she said as calmly as she could, “I understand how you feel. I don’t like doctors, either. Can’t stand them, in fact. All that poking and prodding…” She gave a little shudder. “Sometimes they’re a necessary evil, though, and this may be one of those times. We really do need to get you checked out.”

When he started to protest, she said quickly, “It’ll be all right. We’ll just go and get it over with. I would have taken you last night, but a tree fell across the road and it was too large for me to move by myself. That’s why I brought you here. But the road’s probably been cleared by now, so after breakfast, we should head into town.”

“I don’t need a doctor. I’m not injured.” At least he sounded calmer now. He picked up the chair and sat back down at the table. After a moment, he resumed eating as if his previous eruption had never happened. He glanced over at her. “I’m sorry.”

“No harm done.” Claudia shrugged, but her heart was still thumping against her chest. She wasn’t sure how to proceed. Obviously, he had a thing about doctors. Okay, fine. But he couldn't stay here. She had to somehow get that point across without setting him off again.

"Please don't be afraid," he said.

It was hard to stay agitated when he looked at her that way. So concerned. So innocent. So...genuinely earnest.

Who was this guy?

Claudia mustered a smile. "Look...I appreciate your situation. I do. But you have to see a doctor. Amnesia doesn't just happen out of the blue. You may have a head injury and I'm not...equipped to handle any of this." Although there was such a thing as hysterical amnesia and he'd certainly seemed agitated a moment ago.

But, whatever, she wasn't equipped to handle a mental breakdown, either. She would leave his diagnosis to the professionals. Right now, she needed be done with this whole uncomfortable situation. The longer he stayed, the easier it was to get drawn into his back story, whatever that was.

As if reading her thoughts, his hand crept to the side of his neck where Claudia had spotted the series of bruises earlier.

She watched him for a moment, telling herself not to ask but finding she couldn't resist. "Does your neck hurt?"

"Hurt? No..."

"Is it sore?"

He shook his head.

She bit her lip, wondering how far she should push it. "I saw the bruises on your neck. Is that where they stuck the needles in?"

"Needles…?"

"You said last night that the needles hurt. I assume you meant from injections. It's possible you're on some sort of medication." Another thought struck her. "Or you may have been drugged. That could explain the amnesia, and it's all the more reason why we have to get you to a doctor."

He looked on the verge of arguing with her again, then he subsided with a brief nod. "If that's what you want…Claudia."

But the look he gave her was vaguely reproachful, as if he knew she planned to abandon him as soon as they got into town.

Well, so what? she thought defensively. What did he expect from her?

"It's for the best," she said, refusing to feel guilty about her decision.

She also refused to meet his gaze for the rest of the meal.

Chapter Twelve

After breakfast, Jack asked if he could take a walk before they headed into town. Claudia was a little suspicious but didn't see how she could forbid him from going outside. And, anyway, even if he did take off, would that be so bad? Wasn't the plan to have someone else take him off her hands as quickly as possible?

While his disappearance might solve her immediate problem, she still had the big picture to consider. Chances were good the mysterious organization that had ordered the hit on Dr. Lasher was still gunning for her. She'd seen the killer and she'd also been privy to a good deal of her mentor's research, although not as much as the bad guys might think. Still, as far as they were concerned, she was a loose cannon and would probably remain a hunted woman for the rest of her life. Getting rid of Jack Maddox wasn't going to change that.

What if he really had been sent to protect her?

Maybe something had happened along the way to cause him to lose his memory. In which case, Claudia would be a fool to send him away.

On the other hand, he could *be* one of the bad guys and for whatever reason, was playing her until the time came to kill her.

Good guy, bad guy. Guardian, killer.

Mental patient.

Which was he?

She put a hand to her forehead. All the back and forth emotions were eating away at her confidence, and that was the last thing she needed—to doubt her own instincts. The only safe course of action was to follow through with her initial plan. Take him into town and make him someone else's problem.

Besides, Jack Maddox as protector made about as much sense this morning as it had last night. How could he have been sent here to guard her when no one knew where she was? Her parents were dead, she had no siblings and she'd cut off all ties with friends and colleagues. Not even the police knew where she'd fled to.

Claudia supposed he could have used his precognitive abilities—if he truly had them—to track her down, but the question remained as to how he'd even known about her. The logical—and far more disturbing—explanation was that he had some connection to Dr. Lasher and his research. And that brought her straight back to the men who wanted her dead. *Was he one of them?*

By this time, her nerves were so tautly strung, she felt as if she might fly into a million pieces as she watched him from the window. He stood at the bottom of the porch steps with his back to the cabin, head cocked and tilted skyward, as if listening intently for some distant sound or signal.

Claudia thought of the voice inside her head the night before and shuddered.

Did he hear that same, silent command? Was he trying to communicate with someone?

That notion was not at all comforting and Claudia quickly scanned the countryside. Like creeping paranoia, a layer of fog slid down from the hills, providing excellent ground cover for whatever predators might lie in wait.

So acute was her sense of dread at that moment, her breath quickened and a cold chill descended over her. She swallowed hard and forced herself to draw a few relaxing breaths as she turned away from the window.

Stay calm. Just think this thing through.

She'd eluded Dr. Lasher's killers for two whole years because, even in her darkest hours, she'd managed to keep a clear head. Panic was her enemy. It could make her careless and irrational. Right now, her greatest ally was a calm resolve. That, and the revolver in her sweater pocket. A little information wouldn't hurt, either.

Maybe instead of pondering endlessly on the situation, she should get proactive, do a little research. And there was no better place to start digging than the Internet.

After she logged on, she checked her e-mail to see if there were any client emergencies. Even in the face of her current predicament, she took her job very seriously because it was her only means of support. To stay hidden, one needed a steady source of cash. She had savings, but those funds would quickly get eaten up if her income was cut off.

Satisfied there were no crashed servers or hacked e-mail accounts to deal with, she went to her favorite news site and scanned the local headlines for any mention of an accident the previous night. She searched for anything that might give her a clue as to where Jack Maddox had come from and where he'd been going when he ran out in front of her car.

She found nothing. No accident. No escaped mental patient or convict. Nothing. Even a Google search of his name proved fruitless.

Claudia stared at the screen for a moment, then typed in *Coronet Blue,* the phrase he'd mentioned the night before. When she hit the search button, the number of links that came up surprised her. Clicking on the first link, she anxiously skimmed the page. Then she scrolled to the top and read the content more thoroughly. Afterward, she sat back and stared at the screen some more.

At least one question about Jack Maddox had been answered. Claudia now knew the significance of *Coronet Blue.*

It was beginning to seem as if the man really did suffer from a mental disorder. Delusions of grandeur, perhaps.

Delusions of some sort, for sure.

Chapter Thirteen

The fog rolling down from the higher elevations was cold and damp, but despite his lightweight clothing, Jack barely noticed the chill. He tilted his head skyward and closed his eyes as the mist settled like gossamer over his face. The morning was so still and silent, he could hear the slight rustle of leaves as a hawk took flight from a treetop.

So this was freedom.

He drew a deep breath. *Clean. So clean.* He wanted to drink it in forever.

The moisture on his face was cold and bracing, and he held out a hand to collect water droplets in his palm. He had no memory of mist and yet he knew what it was.

Tilting his head, he listened to the babble of a nearby brook. He couldn't remember ever having waded in a mountain stream, and yet he knew the sound of trickling water over rock, knew the icy nip against his bare feet.

What *did* he remember?

His hands clamped around metal bars. The sting of the needles in his neck. The voice of his tormenter goading him.

"You should be grateful for everything I've done for you. I raised you as my own, gave you the opportunity for greatness, and what do I get in return?"

Jack pressed his fingertips to his suddenly throbbing temples.

"Because of me, your abilities have been maximized *to the fullest."*

"But I just want to be normal."

"Normal! Don't you understand? You'll never be normal. There's no going back. You've become a member of a very elite group. You've been given an extraordinary opportunity and for that you repay me with betrayal. Well, we'll see how you like it at the Facility. No one has ever escaped from there..."

The Facility.

The pounding in Jack's head intensified. For a moment, the world spun out of control and he stumbled, almost losing his balance before he could grab the porch railing to regain his equilibrium.

Just as quickly as it had come, the memory faded, leaving him with only faint traces of what had been there before. But already new information was being imprinted over those traces. He closed his eyes and called forth the image of Claudia that had drawn him to her.

Standing with her back to the edge of a cliff, she

reached out to him, and then her arms flailed wildly as she lost her footing. She screamed his name and he lunged toward her.

For a split second—for an eternity—their gazes clung before she toppled backward and disappeared.

Chapter Fourteen

When Jack came back into the house, he went straight over to the fireplace to warm his hands. Claudia caught only a brief glimpse of his face, but she thought he definitely looked troubled.

As well you should. I'm on to you, buddy.

Although if her hunch was right, he had his own problems and she really did feel bad for him. God only knew what had put him in such an unstable state.

Still, she wasn't about to let down her guard, even in the face of what she had discovered. She remained at her desk, but swiveled her chair so that she could watch him. The gun stayed in her pocket, within easy reach, but she wasn't really afraid of him anymore.

What did she feel?

A little devastated, to be honest, because he wasn't the protector he'd professed himself to be. Just a poor guy caught up in his own delusions.

Until that Google search, Claudia hadn't realized how much she'd been hoping he would turn out to be one of the good guys. She'd had no idea how utterly alone and abandoned she could feel until she found out the truth. Which was crazy because she'd been on her own for a long time. She knew no one was coming to her rescue. This was it. This was her life now.

"I've been on the Internet this morning," she said in a conversational tone. "And I've turned up some pretty interesting information."

He turned to face her, his gaze going to the desk behind her. "You used the computer?"

"That's normally how you get on the Internet," she said. "Do you want to see what I found?"

He hesitated, then nodded, already a little leery of something he'd seen in her eyes or heard in her voice. He walked over to her desk and waited.

"I did a Google search on *Coronet Blue,*" she said.

He didn't offer so much as a flicker of recognition, and Claudia wondered if he'd already forgotten mentioning the phrase to her the night before. He also didn't appear to comprehend what she meant by a Google search.

Made sense. She doubted he'd had access to a computer where he'd been.

"Do you remember talking about *Coronet Blue* last night?" she asked as she returned to the page she'd read a few minutes earlier.

"Yes."

She nodded to the picture of the man who appeared on her screen. "Do you recognize him?"

He knelt beside her as a little frown puckered the skin between his brows. "His name is Michael Alden."

"That's right. Well, sort of. He's an actor. Michael Alden is the name of the character he played on a TV series that aired back in 1967 called *Coronet Blue.*"

She shot him a sidelong glance but he didn't react. "In the show, Michael had amnesia. All he could remember was running from a group of men intent on killing him, and the words coronet blue." She clicked off the page and turned to him. "You've seen this show, haven't you, Jack?"

He was silent, his gaze glued to the computer screen.

Claudia tried to keep her voice soft and non-threatening. "Wherever you came from, you've obviously been exposed to some old television shows." She thought of his absorption the night before in *The Brady Bunch* episode. "When you came to last night, you remembered that phrase and that's why you thought I was in danger."

He was still staring at the computer screen. He seemed mesmerized, almost as if her voice had sent him into a deep trance.

"Jack?"

He still didn't speak. His eyes were riveted to the monitor, but Claudia had a feeling he wasn't really seeing the screen. She reached out a hand to touch his arm, then thought better of it.

"Hey, are you okay?"

His eyelids fluttered as he seemed to shake himself

out of the trance. He drew a long, shuddering breath. "I've seen him."

"What, you mean Michael Alden? I'm sure you have. On TV, right?"

"No. Here." He touched his fingertip to his temple.

Oh, dear.

Claudia bit her lip. Maybe showing him the image of the actor hadn't been such a hot idea after all, but she'd hoped it would jar his memory. Then she would at least know who he was and what to do with him.

"You've seen this actor in your head?"

"Not the actor. The boy."

"What boy?" Claudia was clueless. What on earth was he talking about?

He lifted his hand and pointed to the computer screen.

Puzzled, she swiveled her chair around. Closing the tab to the *Coronet Blue* site had taken her back to the news site. The image on the screen was of a ten-year-old boy who'd disappeared on a family outing in the woods a few weeks ago. He was one of a handful of youths who'd vanished without a trace in the past several months. Even with all the modern advancements in crime scene investigation, the police and the FBI continued to be stymied by the lack of forensic evidence and eye witness accounts in the cases.

"I've seen the boy," he said again.

There was something so odd about the tone of his voice—even more than his statement—that stirred a deep uneasiness inside Claudia. He'd seen the missing boy? When, where? How was it possible unless…

No!

Oh, God, that was too horrendous to even contemplate.

She tried to take her mind someplace else. Far better to believe that he really did possess precognitive abilities.

Or that he was making the whole thing up.

Or that he was just plain crazy.

Get him out of your house! her mind screamed as all her fears and doubts came flooding back.

Whether he was dangerous or demented or a little of both, Claudia had no idea at that moment. All she knew was that she had to be very careful how she handled him.

She swallowed as the blood in her veins turned to ice. "You saw the boy? Where?"

He tapped his head again.

"You mean like in a vision or a dream?"

He nodded.

Claudia turned back to the screen. The missing child was towheaded and freckle-faced with liquid eyes and a sweet, mischievous smile.

His parents must be going out of their minds.

She could hardly imagine the hell they were in, fearing the worst but clinging to every last vestige of hope.

So many monsters in the world. So very many.

She turned back to Jack. Was he one of them?

She tried to control her panic. "If you know anything about this child, you have to tell the authorities. I'll drive you into town and you can talk to someone at the police department."

His gaze lifted, trapping her with his intensity. "They won't believe me."

Claudia pushed back her chair and rose. "We still have to try. You'll have to find a way to convince them. If you know where this boy is—"

"I don't. Not him."

She sat back down, her heart hammering in her chest. "But you said you've seen him. There must be something you can tell the authorities about his whereabouts."

"I didn't see this one. I saw the other one."

"One of the other missing boys?" Claudia didn't know whether to believe him or not. Nothing he said made much sense.

"He's wearing a blue coat and a red cap…" His voice trailed off as his eyes narrowed. "There's an emblem on the hat." He looked around, grabbed a pen and notepad from her desk and started to frantically sketch. "Like this."

Claudia snatched the notepad from him. "That looks like the Chicago Bulls emblem." She pulled one up on the screen and compared it to his drawing. "Is this it?"

"Yes."

The missing boy in his vision wore a Bulls cap. Yet another connection to her past life in Chicago? Claudia didn't want to think about that right now.

"So where is *this* boy, the one wearing the cap? Who has him and how can we find him?"

Jack tore his gaze from the screen. His eyes were dark, bleak, haunted. "No one has him yet. But they'll come for him soon. And I know where he'll be when they take him. If we don't get to him first…"

A shadow dropped over his features, and Claudia found that her breath was trapped in her throat. She struggled to regain her composure.

He put a hand on her arm. "We have to find him. We have to save him. There's no one else. Just us."

The knot of fear in her stomach was like a lead weight. Was he telling the truth? She had no idea. But at that moment, something in his eyes made her want to give him the benefit of the doubt because this was no longer about her. If a child was about to be taken—a boy who might one day have the same haunted look in his eyes as this stranger—she had to do everything in her power to save him.

She shoved the notepad back into his hands. "Can you draw the child?"

He took the pad and she watched in fascination as his hand moved over the paper. When he was finished, he handed it back to her and she stared down at the image. This boy had dark hair, dark eyes, a scar above his right eyebrow. He looked to be around the same age as the missing boy in the photograph. Their features were as different as night and day, and yet, if she could believe Jack, they were both targets of a monster.

"This is him? The kid in your vision?"

"Yes."

She gave him a hard, penetrating look. "If you're lying to me about this…"

"I'm telling you the truth," he said as he put a hand to the side of his neck. "If we don't find him in time…" His voice dropped. "He could end up like me."

Chapter Fifteen

Tense and strangely excited, Claudia gripped the wheel as the SUV glided down a hill and rounded a sharp curve. They passed the spot where the tree had come down the night before, and she slowed for the crewmen who were still busy with chainsaws at the side of the road.

"Do we even know where we're going?" she asked as she turned on the wipers to clear the layer of mist that settled over the windshield.

Jack thought for a moment. "West."

She shot him an uneasy glance. Ever since they'd left the cabin, his behavior had been odd, even for him. He'd withdrawn even deeper into his own thoughts and Claudia didn't have a clue what was going on inside his head. She wasn't at all sure she wanted to know.

At least heading west would take them into Rapid City. Once there, she could decide what to do.

She knew what she *should* do. Drive straight to the

police department. If Jack really did have information about a missing child—or rather a child who was about to go missing—the authorities needed to be alerted.

But he was right. Such a warning posed a big problem. Would the police give him the benefit of the doubt or would they be all too willing to smack the crazy label on him the way she'd done?

He is crazy, a little voice in her head argued as she gave him a sidelong scrutiny. *Has to be. Don't believe it? Just take stock:*

Dashing into the middle of the road in a rainstorm—crazy.

Insisting he had come to save her—crazy.

Believing he was a character from an old TV show—crazy out the wazoo.

Claiming he had precognitive abilities—not so crazy, but the authorities wouldn't see it that way. If they didn't ship him off to a psychiatric ward, they'd at least hold him for questioning on the chance that he might actually know something about the disappearances. In the meantime, if he was telling the truth, if he really had seen a vision about the next kidnapping, time was of the essence and going to the police might be the worst thing they could possibly do.

How did I get myself into this mess? Claudia silently bemoaned.

But even as she cursed herself for being so gullible, she also felt a curious exhilaration, as if she were on the verge of a thrilling discovery. Maybe it was time to take a few chances and trust that her luck hadn't yet run out altogether.

She risked another glance at Jack and caught him staring back at her. The look on his face—those dark, fathomless eyes—quickened her breath and she quickly averted her gaze back to the road.

The day was utterly still with mist clinging to the treetops and swirling like a dancer's filmy skirt around the car. The hushed softness cocooned them in lush velvet, and for a moment, it seemed to Claudia that they had left the road and were floating in some esoteric, dreamlike world. Then the tires thundered across a wooden bridge and brought her rudely back to earth.

She sat rigid in the seat, eyes darting occasionally to the rearview mirror. The closer they got to Rapid City, the tenser she became, and her hands tightened on the wheel in an agony of indecision. *What to do, what to do?*

Even as they entered the city limits, she still vacillated. She knew exactly where the police station was located because she'd pinpointed it, along with the nearest hospital, as soon as she arrived in the area. She could head to either of those places right now, drop off Jack Maddox and just keep driving.

Maybe she wouldn't even go back to the cabin. She'd stashed emergency cash and supplies in various locations. She could disappear yet again, start over somewhere else, forget about the stranger and his outlandish claim that a child was in danger.

But what if he was telling the truth?

What if another boy really was about to be taken… and she and Jack were the only ones who could stop the kidnapping?

As preposterous as it sounded, Claudia couldn't quite dismiss the possibility. Something about that flash of horror in Jack's eyes…the fear and desperation in his voice…

If we don't stop them, he could end up like me.

A man who didn't like memories.

The bottom of her stomach dropped as the road dipped and swelled beneath them. She closed her eyes briefly and let out a breath. No matter how much she might wish to, she couldn't ignore Jack's claim. Not when a child might be involved. Not when Jack himself seemed so tormented.

Despite all her fears, Claudia knew she had to see this through. She had no choice. But she would be on guard every second. If he tried anything, she was armed and fully prepared to take him down.

As if reading her thoughts, he turned his head slowly and their gazes met yet again. Claudia felt that same eerie prickle of recognition.

Who was he and why did she feel so drawn to him?

Maybe it's just the loneliness, she tried to convince herself.

She'd been on her own for a long time, even before her move to the Black Hills. Her father had died when she was a child, her mother during Claudia's first year of college. She was accustomed to the solitude. Loneliness had been a part of her life for as long as she could remember, and she'd learned how to keep the worst of it at bay. But a stranger's abrupt arrival in her life had opened a door, painfully reminding her that self-reliance—no matter how necessary—wasn't always enough.

She drew another breath, letting her decision sink in. Where all this was headed, she had no idea. But she had the uncanny feeling that it was out of her hands now. All of it. Her destiny had already been altered by the man sitting beside her.

"Where to now?" she asked softly as she navigated the streets.

He said nothing for a moment as his gaze drifted from hers to the surrounding scenery. "Southwest. Toward the faces."

She stared at him in surprise as they pulled up to a traffic light. "Faces? You mean Mount Rushmore?"

He seemed to blank out for a moment as he closed his eyes and she saw him shudder. The traffic noises faded, and it seemed to Claudia that the world came to a complete stop along with the vehicle.

She waited, breathless, as a chill lifted the hair at her nape. "What's wrong? What else do you see?" She spoke hesitantly, reluctant to admit, even with her history, that he had the power to foresee future events. Because if he really had come to save her—

She glanced away. Maybe she wasn't ready to accept that quite yet.

He took another moment, then opened his eyes, staring straight ahead. "We need to hurry."

That was it. That was all he said, but something in his tone instilled a deep sense of urgency in Claudia. Without thinking, she tromped the accelerator and the vehicle blasted through the intersection as if the devil himself was on their heels.

Glancing in the rearview mirror yet again, she saw that the road behind them was clear.

Maybe because the devil is right here in the car with me.

CLAUDIA HAD BEEN TO Mount Rushmore a couple of times when she first moved to the area, and though it had never been at the top of her list of places to visit and things to do before she died, she'd been struck by the rugged beauty and grandeur of the sculpture against the majestic backdrop of pristine mountain vistas and dense coniferous forests.

After her first visit, she'd made a point of reading up on the history and had come across a few fascinating details, such as the secret chamber behind the sculpture and the nearby unexplored caverns. She supposed being a hunted woman had naturally ignited her interest in hiding places.

She climbed out of the car and shivered in the chilly air as she tugged on her thermal gloves. Since Jack had nothing to ward off the damp cold except a lightweight jacket, she felt a bit guilty for bundling up. But not shamed enough to shed any of her warm layers. What would be the point in both of them freezing? Resolutely, she pulled up the hood of her parka.

In spite of the unfavorable viewing conditions, they encountered a steady stream of tourists as they walked through the entrance and made their way past the gift shops and food center. As they emerged from the Hall of Flags onto the wide Grand View Terrace, Claudia's gaze darted about for a ten-year-old boy in a blue coat and red cap, but there were no kids of any age or gender among the clusters of sightseers that mingled along the wall and railing.

The mist over the mountain was so thick only a portion of the presidents could be seen from the terrace, but Claudia barely noticed. She focused her attention instead on the series of paved and elevated trails that wound around the base of the mountain and through the lush ponderosa forest. If a boy in a blue coat and red cap was down there somewhere, she couldn't spot him.

She turned back to Jack. "What do we do now? Are you sure this is where he'll be?"

"Yes." He walked to the wall and glanced out over the valley toward the monument.

"Do you have any idea where we should start looking for him?" she asked, trying to quash the nervous jitters in her stomach. Was she really doing this? Putting her life on the line for a complete stranger? For a claim that might not even have a basis in reality?

Apparently, she was.

Jack's gaze rested on the monument and he frowned. "Is there a way we can get closer?"

"You mean closer to the faces? We can walk the Presidents Trail. That'll put us right under the monument at some point." Claudia gestured toward the side of the terrace. "There's an elevator or we can take the stairs down to the visitor's center…hey!"

Before she could even complete her explanation, he was already heading toward the stairs and she had to hurry to catch up with him. She had long legs, but there was no way she could match his stride without breaking into a trot.

At the bottom of the stairs, they made their way through the tourists milling around the visitors' center and those moseying toward the museum, then set out through the dripping trees.

The crowds soon thinned. Maybe it was the thick fog or the stillness of the preternatural forest, but Claudia experienced a strange sense of foreboding. No one knew they were there, but she kept glancing over her shoulder to see if they were being watched or followed.

It's just the eyes, she tried to rationalize. The sculpture had been ingeniously designed to make the eyes appear lifelike. The effect was at once awe-inspiring and a little unsettling. Today, however, the faces could barely be seen through the mist so that was a hard justification to swallow.

Jack's intense focus didn't help her jitters. If ever

she'd seen a man on a mission, it was he. And there she was, blindly following him into only God knew what.

She stumbled, righted herself and kept going. The slope was deceptively steep and the dampness made the wooden boardwalk slippery. The intermittent steps and trail had been designed for a more leisurely hike, but Jack kept up the rapid pace, striding along with that fierce sense of purpose, shoulders slightly forward, head up and alert.

But even in his haste, there was something very stealth-like about his movements. Something very vigilant about the way he cocked his head from time to time, listening to the silence. An owl's plaintive cry floated out from the woods and he paused, waited, then moved on.

Finally, he slowed again as they approached a viewing area right beneath the sculpture. In good weather, one could almost look straight up Washington's nose, but not so much today. The fog was like a shroud, Claudia thought with a shudder.

As Jack studied their surroundings, she took the opportunity to observe him. He seemed so different out here, almost catlike in the slinky, predatory way he moved. The metamorphosis was truly stunning. Back at the cabin, he'd come across as confused and delusional, a man balancing on that thin tightrope of sanity. Out here, he appeared in his element. He stood taller, straighter, cloaked in an air of quiet confidence.

A puzzle wrapped in a mystery, Claudia thought.

She couldn't tear her gaze off him.

Shoving her hands into her pockets, she huddled inside her coat. She was freezing, but in spite of his inadequate clothing, Jack seemed unfazed by the weather.

Is the man even human? she wondered.

"What are we doing here?" she asked, trying to keep her teeth from chattering. She stamped her feet to keep warm and to try and burn off some of her nervous energy. But no matter what she did, she couldn't dispel the flutter of anticipation in her stomach and the shiver of awareness that whispered along her backbone.

Here she was, on a potentially foolhardy quest with an enigmatic stranger, and all she felt at that very moment was…what? Attraction? Excitement? The thrill of the hunt?

And some fear. Thank God for that. At least she hadn't completely lost her mind.

"Well?" she prompted when he didn't respond to her question. "What are we doing, Jack? I haven't seen a single kid since we got here."

He still didn't answer. Instead, he rotated his head slowly from side to side, scouring the shrouded scenery. Then he glanced back toward the amphitheater and viewing platform. After a moment, he left the path and took a few steps toward the trees.

"Hey, come on now, you're not supposed to do that," Claudia said as she pointed to a sign that advised visitors to stay on the trail. "You'll have the rangers down here on us."

He didn't even bother to glance back, paying no heed to her warning or the sign. He kept walking and soon disappeared into the thick forest of conifers that grew at the base of the mountain.

"That's just great," Claudia muttered. *See what happens when you throw your lot in with a nut job?*

That strange hush fell over her again as she watched the pale drift of mist through the trees where Jack had vanished. She could smell damp earth and evergreens and last season's rotting leaves. The fecund scent reminded her not of growing things, but of death and decay. Of the approaching winter and her coming hibernation.

Loneliness gnawed at her gut but she tried to ignore it. She had more important things to concentrate on at the moment.

Like wild animals.

Claudia had lived in the woods long enough to be accustomed to wary eyes and the rustle of leaves beneath scurrying paws. But in that eerie vacuum of silence, the sudden crunch of underbrush startled her, and she couldn't help wondering what might be out there. Her imagination took flight as she pictured all sorts of predatory creatures—mythical and otherwise—sneaking up on her. The mist would hide them all. The bears and the mountain lions. The werewolves and vampires and the monsters who preyed on innocent children.

As the seconds ticked by, she grew more nervous. She was used to solitude, but this was different. Something about this place bothered her, and she didn't like being there by herself. They'd encountered very few people on the trail and now that Jack had taken off, she felt exposed and vulnerable in spite of the mist. A sitting duck.

On clear days, the clamor of footsteps on the wooden walkway would have alerted her to anyone approaching, but the fog muffled sound so thoroughly that she was startled when a couple suddenly appeared out of nowhere.

Recovering from her shock, she looked for a boy in their company, but they were alone.

The woman smiled and the man nodded before vanishing back into the haze.

Claudia let out a breath. No bears or werewolves, thank goodness. Just a couple of harmless tourists. She stared after them, rubbing her arms to keep warm.

A few moments later, Jack clamored back onto the walkway, but for some reason, his sudden emergence from the mist didn't faze her. It was almost as if she'd known when and where he would appear, but that was impossible. She wasn't the pre-cog.

Maybe I just have really good hearing, Claudia thought. *Or uncanny instincts.*

She looked at him askance. "Where did you go off to?"

"I needed to reconnoiter."

Reconnoiter? The word jarred Claudia. It wasn't something one heard in everyday life.

Did he still think he was Michael Alden from *Coronet*

Blue? Was this all just a powerful delusion she'd let herself buy into?

And this newfound persona…the toughness, the stealth. Where had that come from? Or was it, too, a part of the delusion?

If so, Claudia had to say, it was pretty damn convincing.

"Why were you…reconnoitering?"

His gaze trapped her for a moment before moving on. But Claudia felt a tingle up her spine just the same. Three words came to mind as she stared up at him: tall, dark and handsome. A cliché had never been more apt.

"The tangos have the advantage because we don't know anything about them," he said. "But we can at least know the terrain."

"Tangos?" she asked almost in dread.

His jaw hardened as he spared her a glance. "The enemy. The people who will come for the boy. We have to be ready for them."

The steely conviction in his voice and the icy determination in his eyes set Claudia's heart to pounding. Maybe this was all a delusion and maybe it wasn't. She could say only one thing with certainty at the moment—Jack Maddox was a strange and powerful enigma. A compelling chameleon, who, in the space of a few short hours, had turned her world upside down.

"I'm glad you're on my side," she murmured, though not loud enough for him to hear. She would definitely not want to cross swords with the man she saw before her. He loomed over her, tall and formidable, and she could do nothing but gawk in awe.

He seemed oblivious to her scrutiny as he blew on his hands to warm them up.

"Here." She took off her wool scarf and tried to drape it around his neck, but he grabbed her hand to stop her. His lightning reaction was so unexpected that Claudia actually jumped.

"What's the matter?" she asked, her breath catching in her throat as his gaze clamped onto hers. His eyes were a deep, deep blue, like shadowed sea water. Mysterious and fathomless. So very dangerous.

"I thought you were—" He said nothing else as he searched her face. He seemed to be waiting, but for what, Claudia had no idea.

Then her mind went to the bruises on his neck and she winced. No wonder he was so jumpy.

He glanced away as he dropped her hand.

Claudia purposefully softened her voice. "It's okay. It's just a scarf. It'll help keep you warm. You need it more than I do. I've got a coat and gloves. You must be freezing."

"I'm used to the cold."

"You are? Maybe that means you're from the area," she said as she tentatively held out the scarf. Although that was hardly a revelation, since he'd been on foot when she found him. He couldn't have gotten far in a freezing downpour and inadequate clothing.

"I don't know what it means." He hesitated, then

bent forward so that she could loop the wool around his neck.

His words sounded haunted and lost, and Claudia caught a glimpse of the same confused man who'd wandered into the path of her car the night before. But the betraying look was gone in an instant as his features hardened and his eyes turned back to steel. The transformation was breathtaking.

We can at least know the terrain.

We have to be ready for them.

Good heavens, Claudia thought. *What have I gotten myself into?*

She was no soldier, nor was she particularly courageous. She'd managed to survive as a hunted woman for the past two years, not from any heroics on her part, but out of sheer desperation.

Still, everything considered, she did have one thing working in her favor. Her survival instinct was pretty damn fearsome these days.

"You keep saying 'they.' What did you see in your vision?" she asked nervously. "How many will come for him?"

"Maybe one, maybe many—" He stopped, his eyes sweeping the countryside, and then he went on. "We have to be prepared."

Maybe one, maybe many. That wasn't much comfort.

Claudia shivered.

"Don't worry," he said. "They won't come today."

"How do you know?"

He tilted his head to the veiled monument. "Because you can't see the faces."

Claudia glanced up through the tree branches. The fog was a thick, gray sheet pierced through in places by dark green boughs. "So?"

He made a little gesture of impatience. "When I saw the boy, I could also clearly see the faces behind him. There was no mist." He paused again, frowning, as if trying to call forth other details of the vision. "And I saw light in the eyes."

"In the presidents' eyes? Oh, I know what that is," Claudia said excitedly. "I read somewhere that the pupil of each eye is a shaft of granite. When sunlight shines on the flat end, the eyes appear to twinkle." She grew even more animated. "If you can see light in the eyes, then that must mean the sun is shining directly on the monument when the boy is taken."

He slanted a quick look of surprise. "That makes sense."

"So what we have to figure out is the angle of the light. Then we can pinpoint the location." Claudia turned and dipped her head toward the terrace and amphitheater. "It has to be back that way or else you wouldn't get the 'twinkle' effect in the eyes." She glanced up at the monument. "See what I mean?"

He followed her gaze. "Yes."

"Then we should probably head back, don't you think? We can retrace our steps or follow the trail all the way around to the other side. That'll put us closer to the parking garage." She stopped and studied him for a moment. "I don't know how these things work...the visions, I mean, but if you can remember exactly how the monument is positioned behind the boy, it shouldn't be too hard to figure out the location."

A little silence.

He stared down at her, something hard and cold gleaming in his eyes. Something that tingled the back of Claudia's neck.

"What is it?" she asked quickly.

"You go back. I'm not finished here yet."

"What do you mean? What else is there to do?"

"Just go back."

His insistence, along with his demeanor, was very disconcerting. Suddenly, Claudia was truly afraid of what he might be up to.

She looked at him with open suspicion. "What are you going to do? What aren't you telling me?"

The dark eyes were inscrutable beneath the black brows. "It's like I said before. Our best defense is to know the terrain."

"So you're going to reconnoiter some more? Maybe I should come with you. I need to know the area, too, don't I?"

Another pause. "It's better if I go alone. Go back and warm up. I'll be there soon."

Claudia didn't particularly care for his dismissive tone, and she told herself she should just end the whole thing right then and there. Bid him *adios* and be done with the whole mess.

But instead she found herself asking, "How long will you be?"

"Not long."

"And that's it? That's all you're going to tell me?"

There was nothing dismissive about the way he stared down at her now. His eyes drew her in, made her want to believe him when she knew she should just walk away.

He said her name.

A little thrill shot up her spine. "Yes?"

Even her voice held a faint quiver. This was so not like her. What was happening here? Where was the kick-ass fugitive who'd eluded a brutal killer all on her own for two whole years?

There were no saviors and protectors. Even in her old life, Claudia had never been the type to rely on anyone else. And she'd never believed in fairy tales. She was smarter and much more sophisticated than that. Or at least…she'd always thought so.

This behavior…the trembling knees, the dry mouth, the thumping heartbeat…this was not her.

His gaze deepened. "I need you to trust me."

No! Claudia wanted to scream. *I don't want to trust you. Why should I? I don't know anything about you. I shouldn't even be here with you.*

But those eyes…

God, those incredible eyes made her want to believe all sorts of impossible things.

She hoped none of that showed on her face, but just in case, she tore her gaze away and took a step back from him. "All right, look. I'll go find some hot coffee," she said, in what she hoped was a perfectly normal tone. "I'll meet you back on the terrace. If you're not there in half an hour, I'm leaving without you."

"Then I'll be there."

"You'd better be."

She turned to go, but he caught her arm and she slowly faced him. For a moment, she could say nothing, and then she moistened her lips and strove for a careless, impatient tone. "What now?"

He removed the scarf from his neck and wrapped it carefully around her throat. "There."

His fingers brushed against the underside of her jaw, shocking her, and Claudia said sharply, "Thanks."

What it her imagination, or had his fingers lingered? Was it only wishful thinking, or had she seen a flash of desire in those dark, soulful eyes?

And then a brief smile flickered across his face and for a split second, Claudia forgot how to breathe.

Chapter Sixteen

The coffee helped revive Claudia, but the warmth was only a momentary reprieve. As she waited on the terrace, she could feel the cold seeping through her coat and with it, a certainty that something was very wrong. Jack should have been back before now. Where on earth was he? Had he run into trouble?

Maybe he'd been mistaken about sunlight on the faces in his vision. Maybe this really was the day the kidnapping would take place, and he was down there right now, dealing with the hostile "tangos" on his own.

Or…maybe he'd just up and run off, leaving her high and dry.

Wouldn't be the first time she'd been stood up. Taking into account her old life, nothing much would surprise Claudia when it came to Jack Maddox. Everything about him was so truly bizarre, she had no measuring stick. Her brain told her what she should do, but her gut told her something else.

Logically, she knew she shouldn't trust him—or

anyone—and yet she couldn't deny there was an attraction. She was drawn to him. What that meant or where it would lead, she had no idea. Only that when she gazed into those blue eyes, she wanted more than anything to believe him. She desperately needed for him to be one of the good guys.

But apart from her own personal wants and needs, she wouldn't, *couldn't* discount his claim about the impending kidnapping for two very important reasons: the tormented look on his face when he hinted at what might happen to the boy and Claudia's own belief in precognition.

Her work with the REGs had left little room for doubt. Like Dr. Lasher, she'd come to accept that precognition was very much a natural human ability similar to intuition and instinct, all primal thought processes that had once been tied directly to the survival of the human species.

Given all that, she couldn't disregard the validity of Jack's visions. If there was a chance, no matter how remote, that she could help save a child, then she would move heaven and earth to do so. She wouldn't be able to live with herself if another boy disappeared and she'd done nothing to stop it.

So many ifs. So many questions.

Growing more agitated by the moment, Claudia checked the time yet again. She'd told Jack she would wait on the viewing terrace for half an hour, but it had now been over forty-five minutes. Maybe he really wasn't coming back. Or maybe he'd misunderstood their rendezvous point and he was waiting for her at the car.

As Claudia took another look around, she caught sight of a man coming through the columns onto the terrace. His size captured her attention first. He looked behemoth, well over six-three with broad shoulders buried beneath a sleek, black parka. He wore the hood pulled down low over his face and though he had his head turned away, Claudia could see a bit of his profile.

The shock of recognition was like a physical blow. She'd seen that face before—just a devastating glimpse—as the elevator doors slid closed at the laboratory mere moments before she'd found Dr. Lasher's body.

And now his killer had found her.

Hide!

Claudia reacted to her nightmarish terror with pure instinct and adrenaline. She dove behind one of the huge pillars and pressed her back into the stone. Closing her eyes, she gasped for breath as she tried to control her thundering heartbeat.

No, no, no!

It couldn't be.

She'd dreamed of and dreaded this moment for two long years. Every night when she closed her eyes, she saw that face in her sleep. Each time she went out in public, she kept watch behind her back and around every street corner for that terrifying visage.

And now there he was…

So very close…

Had he seen her? She didn't think so. His head had been turned away. And anyway, her hair was longer now and she had on sunglasses. To her eyes, the reflection she saw in the mirror these days barely resembled the short-haired, intense research assistant she'd long left behind in Chicago.

But there had to be a reason he'd turned up so fortuitously on the terrace. Someone must have tipped him off. Someone like Jack Maddox.

I need you to trust me.

Trust you, my ass, Claudia thought bitterly.

To think that she'd come so close to doing exactly that. This was a big wake-up call. If ever she'd needed a reminder that she should place faith in no one but herself, this was it. Betrayal was a real bitch.

But after a moment of shock and fright, reason began to seep back in. Maybe it wasn't even the same man. Maybe she'd only imagined the similarity. After all, she hadn't even gotten a good look at his face—now or two years ago. In all likelihood, he was just some tourist who'd happened along at a time when her defenses were already on high alert. That had to be it. She'd once again let her imagination get the better of her.

Claudia braced herself for another look. Easing along the width of the column, she glanced around the edge, her gaze sweeping over the terrace. She saw him at once. His size made him easy to pick out in a crowd, and her eyes went straight to the black parka as if he were wearing a homing device.

He stood at the wall with a pair of binoculars, but rather than gazing toward the mist-shrouded monument, he'd trained the lenses downward, as if he were searching along the trails.

For her?

Okay, no conclusion-jumping, Claudia warned herself. She had to be careful not to let her imagination incite irrational fear. Panic would do her no good. She had to stay calm and in control even though her heart was beating in her throat.

Lots of people brought binoculars to Mount Rushmore. No big deal. It didn't mean anything.

Biting her lips together to keep them from trembling, Claudia watched him from her hiding place. As he continued to comb the countryside, he took out a cell phone and lifted it to his ear. When he turned slightly, she caught another glimpse of his profile before she jerked back and flattened herself against the stone column.

Easy. No cause for alarm just because he's talking on a cell phone.

But in spite of her resolve, Claudia was panicking. Big time.

Maybe she'd seen the man before, maybe she hadn't. Maybe he was Dr. Lasher's killer and maybe he wasn't. She couldn't afford to take any chances. If she'd learned anything since she'd gone into hiding it was to listen to her internal warning system. Something about the man on the terrace had set off all kinds of bells, and now she had to figure out what to do.

If she tried to exit through the Hall of Flags, he might spot her. But she couldn't stay where she was indefinitely. She was an easy target on the terrace.

She cast about frantically for a means of escape. The steps that led down to the trails were off to her right. To get to them, she'd be out in the open for a couple of seconds, completely exposed, but if she kept her head and timed it just so…

Inching around the column, she took another quick peek. The man was heading straight for her!

She flinched back, flattening herself against the wall, sick with fear. Even head on, she hadn't been able to see his features clearly because the hood of his parka was pulled so low over his face and his head was bowed.

Claudia wished she could see his hair. The man in the elevator had been a redhead, and he'd had the most piercing blue eyes she'd ever looked into. He'd been smiling, too, as if he'd found his brutal encounter with Dr. Lasher quite pleasant.

She shivered as she remembered that smile, those eyes, that hair.

All that blood.

She itched to steal another glance, but she didn't dare. If the sun had been shining, she might have been able to gauge his approach by his looming shadow, but the day was too overcast and she couldn't tell how close he was.

Cocking her head, she listened for his footsteps. They were almost upon her before she heard them. And then the sound of his voice caused her to jump.

She pressed a hand to her mouth to suppress an involuntary gasp. But he wasn't talking to her. He was still on the phone, speaking in a hushed voice, as if wary of being overheard. Claudia couldn't make out the words, nor could she tell anything from his tone. All she knew was that he was very close. He came to a stop right beside the column where she was hidden. Another step and he would have seen her for sure.

Her shoulder blades were taut with terror as she pressed herself even harder into the stone and slid around to the other side. She still wanted to believe that she was overreacting. Prayed that she was seeing things. But better safe than sorry, always.

The man remained beside the column for a moment or two before he moved away. Only when his voice and footsteps faded did Claudia dare sneak another look. He was nowhere in sight.

Frantically, she scanned the terrace. He wasn't there.

Her gaze moved to the Hall of Flags. Had he left the same way he'd come in? Had he ducked into the gift shop or food center, maybe?

She couldn't wait around to find out. Surveying the terrace one last time, she dashed toward the stairs.

Winged by fear, she tore down the trail, slipping and stumbling in her haste and glancing over her shoulder for any sign of pursuit.

When she'd been to the monument in warmer weather, the trails had been crowded with visitors, making it easier to blend in. Today that wasn't the case and she was grateful for the fog as camouflage. It was nearly waist-high in places, sliding down from the hills like a slow-moving avalanche. Even through binoculars, she would be hard to spot.

At the sound of a snapping twig, she stopped dead, gripped by a paralyzing fear. She was so spooked by this time, she barely managed to suppress the scream that rose to her throat a mere split second before Jack appeared like a phantom beside her.

Claudia didn't utter a word, but he must have seen the terror on her face. He was around her in a flash, putting himself between her and the trail back to the terrace. The trained reaction was so incongruent to her previous thoughts of betrayal that she couldn't quite process it. Couldn't quite come to terms with the relief that rushed through her.

"Something's happened." His gaze inspected the scenery around them, then came quickly back to her. "What is it?"

Did she dare trust him?

All she had to go on were her instincts, and for whatever reason, he had never set off the same kind of alarm bells as the man on the terrace. Claudia had to believe that meant something, as did the sheer joy she felt at the very sight of him. And he did seem more than willing to put himself between her and danger. That in itself was pretty overwhelming.

"I saw a man on the viewing terrace just now," she said in a breathless rush. "He looked like someone from my past."

Jack's body seemed to tense, like an arrow pulled from a tautly strung bow, and he appeared taller than ever. Claudia suddenly had a mental image of a face-off between him and the man on the terrace. Jack would be outsized, but at that moment, she would put money on lean, supple quickness over sheer bulk. But maybe that was because she really did believe in fairy tales. Or desperately wanted to.

"Who is he?" Jack's voice was deep, rough, edged with anger.

Claudia forced the tell-tale quiver from her own throat. "It was probably nothing, just my imagination—"

"But you're afraid of him." A statement not a question.

"If he's who I think he is, yes. But like I said, I may be overreacting. Seeing things or whatever. It's just… I don't know for sure. And I can't take a chance on being seen. I have to get out of here somehow. But if we go back the way we came, he could be waiting for me."

"Then we'll find another way back to the car." Jack stepped off the trail and took her hand to pull her up beside him. "You don't need to worry. I won't let that man hurt you. I won't let anyone hurt you."

Claudia tried to muster up some confidence. "I'd like to believe you, but if that man is from my past, you have no idea what we're up against."

"Neither does he," Jack said.

Chapter Seventeen

Skirting the trail and most of the crowds, they finally made it back to the parking garage without incident, but it wasn't until they were well away from the monument that either of them relaxed. And even then, Claudia had very little to say.

Jack desperately needed to know about the man she'd seen on the terrace, but he didn't press her to talk. If he had any chance at all of gaining her trust, he couldn't overplay his hand. He may have won a slim battle back on the trail, but he knew she still had doubts. Who could blame her? He had no memory of who he really was or where he'd come from. All he knew for sure was that she was in danger. They both were. And if they didn't find the boy in time, he would end up like Jack.

He closed his eyes, hearing his tormenter's voice.

Your abilities have been maximized to the fullest. There's no going back. Ever.

He tried to shove the taunt to the farthest reaches of

his mind as he turned to stare out the window. The hills were black with evergreens, the valleys swathed in swirling mist. If he lowered the window, he would be able to smell pine, moss and dying leaves. The scent of winter. Already, he could feel the chill in his bones as he watched the drift of a lone hawk against the slate sky.

Such a strange countryside, he thought.

This place was not his home. He somehow knew that. And yet the shadowed gorges and thick bands of firs called forth something primal within him. Something was welling inside him, a ferocious call to arms that he didn't fully understand.

He glanced down at his hands, turned them over, studying the lines and creases in his palms. He could kill with those hands to survive. He knew that. He *would* kill to save Claudia. He knew that, too.

He couldn't explain the bond between them any more than he could deny it. They were connected. He accepted it without question. And he would do whatever it took to keep her safe, even sacrifice his own life. Not out of a false sense of heroics, but because he could do nothing else. She was the reason he was here. She was the reason he *was.*

He turned to examine her profile and her answering gaze was tentative. "What?"

"I need to know about the man you saw back at the faces. Why were you so afraid of him?"

A tiny pulse beat at her temple. "I'd rather not talk about it."

"Why?"

"Because I don't like thinking about my past. And because…" She trailed off and bit her lip. "Just because."

"You still don't trust me."

She shrugged. "No, I do. Sort of."

"I came here to save you," he said.

She gave him an unhappy look. "So you keep reminding me. But just because you say it enough times doesn't mean I'm actually going to believe you. I mean, come on. This whole situation is a bit…"

He waited.

"Crazy."

"Why do you say that?"

She spared another glance. "Who wouldn't say that?"

"Claudia."

Reluctantly, she looked at him. "Yeah?"

"Put aside everything else for a moment. Just tell me about this man."

She sighed in frustration. "Why can't you just leave it alone for now? We can talk about it later."

"We need to talk about it now. There may not be a lot of time left."

"Oh, well, that makes me feel ever so much better." She grimaced, then shot him a frustrated glance. "Look, this is hard for me. You just show up out of the blue and expect me to drop all my defenses when, for all I know, you were the one who told that man we'd be at the monument today."

He lifted a brow. “When would I have done that?”

“I don’t know. Maybe you’re also a telepath.” She cracked a weak smile, but Jack didn’t see anything funny about the suggestion.

“I’m not a telepath.”

“Don’t be so literal. It was a joke, okay? Although sometimes you do seem like you can read my mind. It creeps me out if you want to know the truth.”

“I wish I could read your thoughts right now,” he said. “Because I really need to know if the man you saw today is the one who’s been tracking you.”

“*Tracking* me? Good God, when you put it that way…” He saw her shudder, then her voice cracked and grew suspicious. “How do you know someone is tracking me?”

“You live alone in the woods,” he said. “And your cabin is isolated. It’s not hard to figure out that you’re hiding from something. Or someone. And I know you’re in danger.”

“Yes, but *how* do you know that?” She sounded almost angry. “You never explained it to me. Did you have some sort of vision about me like you did the boy? Is that how *you* tracked me down?”

He turned away for a moment as the image of her death flashed through his head. He replayed in his mind that split second when their gazes clung before she plummeted backward over the cliff.

“I won’t let that happen,” he said.

“What?” When he didn’t answer, she said impatiently, “Tell me about the vision. What did you see?”

"You're in danger. That's all I know. That's all I need to know. And all you need to know is that I'll do whatever I have to do to protect you."

"Why?" she demanded. Her knuckles whitened where she gripped the steering wheel. "Why do you care what happens to me?"

He was at a loss to explain. "Because…I don't have a choice."

"Everyone has a choice. Why should you care whether I live or die? I'm just some stranger to you."

"You're not a stranger."

"I was until last night. You'd never laid eyes on me before then."

"But I know you just the same."

"How? Through your visions?"

He grew pensive, searching for his own answers. "Yes. And that's why I need to know about the man you saw on the viewing terrace. Why won't you tell me who he is and why you're so afraid of him?"

She was very still for a moment. "You don't understand. I've been on my own for a long time. I've had to learn to take care of myself. Putting my trust in someone else is probably just about the dumbest thing I could do."

"Or the smartest."

"Maybe." She slanted a look. "But I guess that all depends on whether you turn out to be the good guy or the bad guy."

He glanced down at his hands. "Maybe I'm a little of both," he muttered.

"Yeah, and that's what worries me most of all, that *you* don't even know."

He looked up and their gazes clung for a moment before she trained her eyes back on the road.

She gestured helplessly with one hand. "I admit, there's a part of me that wants to trust you. I'm not sure why, but it's there. Then I think about the whole situation. The amnesia and all that. You have no idea who you are or where you came from. Or who you might work for. Under the circumstances…" Another helpless flutter. "See my dilemma?"

"Yes. But it doesn't have to be that hard. All you have to do is listen to your instincts. If you can't trust me, trust yourself. That may be the only thing that will save your life."

"I thought you were going to save me." Her voice held a challenge.

"I can only do that if you place your faith in me."

"Oh, boy." She rolled her eyes. "Can we at least skip the melodrama?"

But the protest was half-hearted. He could sense that she wanted to open up to him. Whether she would admit it or not, she was starting to believe in him. He fervently hoped nothing in his past would surface to betray that hard-earned trust.

"Tell me about that man," he pressed as he searched her face. Even in her agitated state, she looked fierce and lovely and vulnerable. He was pretty certain he'd never known anyone like her.

As if reading his thoughts, she scowled at the road. "All right, you win." But the capitulation was reluctant, almost grudging. "I don't know what else to do, so I'll give you the highlights."

"Thank you for that."

She shrugged, then lifted a hand to rub the back of her neck. "Before I moved here I was a research assistant in Chicago for a man named Thomas Lasher. He once worked for the Global Consciousness Project, which is an international group of scientists and researchers that collects data from a network of REGs—random event generators—placed all over the world. The REGs spit out a constant stream of ones and zeros in random fashion. The purpose of the research is to determine whether deviations in the randomness of the number sequences correlates with major world events that engage large numbers of people. Princess Di's death, for instance. Such a finding could suggest the presence of a collective consciousness."

She stopped and gave him an apologetic glance. "Sorry. Did you understand any of that?"

He thought about it and nodded, surprising even himself. "Yes."

"You did?" She couldn't hide her astonishment. "Most people would think it just a bunch of gobbledygook. Back in Chicago, I never could explain to my friends exactly what I did for a living. I used to just tell them I worked with numbers. Most of them thought I was an accountant," she said dryly. "But you aren't most people, are you, Jack?"

"No, and neither are you." He returned her stare until she flinched and glanced away.

"Which feeds right into my paranoia," she said worriedly. "None of this is random, is it? Me, you… here. It can't be a coincidence. Someone is pulling the strings."

"Maybe…I don't know. All I know is that I had to come here." But she had a point. Something had compelled him to that very spot on the road the night before. Whether it was anything more than his visions of her impending death, he couldn't honestly say. "Tell me more about Dr. Lasher."

Her face immediately softened. "It would take the rest of the day to tell you about Dr. Lasher. He was an extraordinary man. Absolutely brilliant. He was an innovator in his field, utterly fearless when it came to taking risks with his career for the sake of something he believed in. I was privileged to have known him, much less worked with him. When I think about what he might have accomplished had he lived…" She was momentarily caught by a wave of emotion, though she tried her hardest to conceal it. But she couldn't quite disguise the telltale quiver in her voice or the sudden sheen in her eyes.

Jack waited silently.

She brushed the back of her hand across her cheek. "Anyway, to make a long story short, Dr. Lasher left the project to pursue his own research, hooked up with some really bad dudes who wanted to exploit his findings and when he refused to cooperate, they sent someone to murder him. And lucky me, I just happened to be at the right place at the right time that night to get a glimpse of the killer."

"And that's how you ended up here? You ran?"

"Not at first, but it soon became clear that the police couldn't protect me. There were some incidents. Strange phone calls, a break-in. Someone following me. Mostly, I think I was being warned. And I also got the distinct impression I was being toyed with. A cat-and-mouse thing. I decided not to wait around for the trap to spring shut on me."

"Was the man you saw that night the same man you saw today?"

"I thought so at first, but the more I look back on it, I'm pretty sure it was just my imagination. I never got a good look at him, that night or today. I think I just over-reacted. Let my nerves get the better of me or something."

Jack watched her closely. "What did he look like, this man?"

"You mean the killer?" Her voice was steady, but he could sense her tension. Her fear. It was almost a tangible thing. "Like I said, I only had a brief glimpse of him. I remember him as huge, a real hulk, but maybe time and fear has added a few inches and pounds." She paused. "You would think a blue-eyed redhead would be fair, but he had this…darkness about him. I can't explain it. It was like there was a perpetual shadow over him or something." She shuddered and gripped the steering wheel.

Jack went completely still. Something she'd said had struck a chord. "You say…he had red hair?"

"Yes. It was a very strange color of red. It reminded me of blood…" She glanced over at him. "What's wrong?"

He couldn't answer. A door had opened in his mind and a memory slipped through.

Someone stood in the shadows just outside his cell. From down a long, dark corridor he could hear the screams. The sound both enraged and terrified him as he tightened his hands around the metal bars.

"Make it stop or I swear to God, I'll—"

"You'll what? Kill me?" A low laugh. "You're in no position to make threats. Besides, in here, I'm God. If you haven't accepted that by now, I'm afraid there isn't much hope." He came out of the shadows, a wiry man with a cruel mouth and tangled, white hair. Such an unassuming figure and yet he wielded a power far greater than life and death.

"Let him go."

He tugged at the lapels of his rumpled lab coat. "In due time. At the moment, you should just enjoy your reprieve. You did, after all, draw the longest straw. Or rather, I drew it for you. But no matter. Let his screams be a lesson to you." He moved closer to the bars. There was something unholy about the hard glitter in his eyes, that taunting smile. "The next time I have to send Red to find you, there won't be enough left of either of you to bring back."

As the image faded, Jack heard another voice inside his head. Not a memory this time, but a softly probing whisper that rose and faded like an ocean tide. It wasn't really a voice, he realized, but more of an impression. Or a thought transference.

Jack?

He glanced over at Claudia. She watched the road, her brows furrowed in deep concentration.

Jack!

The projection was an urgent command, and with it came a strong sense of warning.

"Pull over," he said.

Claudia looked at him in alarm. "Are you sick?"

"Please, just stop the car."

She found a place on the shoulder wide enough to safely pull off the road, and he jumped out while the vehicle was still rolling.

"Hey!"

Striding several feet away, he stood with his back to the car, head tilted to the mountains, his gaze roaming the misty landscape. All was silent. He could hear no sound at all except for his raging blood and the rapid beating of his heart.

The voice came again, softly at first, then stronger, as if a sudden gust of wind had swept aside the fog inside his head. The voice was distinct, forceful and eerily familiar.

Jack? Jack!

He could feel a clenching tension at the back of his neck, so painful he couldn't concentrate. With an effort, he forced his muscles to relax as he tried to empty his mind.

Jack! Where are you?

I'm here...with the girl...

Jack!

A deep, pulsing silencing. And then…

...danger...

The last was nothing more than a wispy impression, and then the voice, the entity, the vision—whatever it was—faded slowly back into the mist.

"Wait," Jack said aloud. "Who are you? Where are you? What do you want from me?"

He hadn't realized until that moment that Claudia had gotten out of the car and followed him. He turned now and found her standing a few feet away, her eyes clouded with confusion. She lifted a hand and tucked a strand of dark blonde hair behind one ear.

For the longest moment, neither of them said anything. Then she drew a breath and glanced off down the valley. "You heard it, too, didn't you?"

He stared at her in shock. "What?"

"You heard…the voice." Her gaze came back to him. "Or whatever it was."

Slowly, he nodded.

"Who is he?" The question was barely audible.

"He?"

She shrugged, but her gaze was very direct. "That's the impression I got. You don't know who he is?"

Jack shook his head.

She moistened her lips and took another breath. "This is all very strange, isn't it?"

"Yes." Her confusion touched him. He had the strongest urge to walk over and put his arms around her, but something held him back. An insecurity that he didn't understand. He wasn't afraid of rejection. He was afraid he might not know the right thing to do.

"What did he say to you?" Claudia asked. He could tell she was trying to cling to her poise, but that tiny tremor in her voice made him want to go to her even more, hold her even tighter.

"Danger."

She lifted a brow. "That's it? That's all he said? Maybe he should try telling us something we don't know." She started a little as he moved toward her. She looked as if she wanted to step back, but instead she held her ground. Her chin came up, a tiny act of defiance. "What's going on, Jack?"

"I don't know."

She hardened her voice. "Why are you here?"

"I've told you why."

"I mean, *why are you here?*"

He continued to walk toward her. "I'm here because of you. I am because of you."

A shadow flickered across her features and then she gave a tiny, bitter laugh. "Oh, the pressure. I hope you're kidding because that's a lot to put on my shoulders. I am only human, after all."

The last was a bit of a taunt and Jack didn't know what to say to that. Now it was he who was lost in confusion. He felt as if he were entering uncharted waters without maps or stars or even instinct to guide him. "Do you want me to leave?"

Her head came up. "Would you, if I said yes?"

"I could disappear, if that's what you want."

"You don't mean that literally, do you?" she asked with an ironic lift of one brow. "Just go poof in a cloud of smoke?"

He allowed himself a brief smile. "I mean, you wouldn't have to know that I'm around."

"You'd just be lurking behind trees, hiding in shadows, stuff like that? You're that good, huh? I'd never even know you were spying on me."

"Protecting you, is how I see it."

She thrust her hands into her pockets. "Even if I don't want you to."

"I don't have a choice. It'll be easier if you just accept that."

"Easier for you, maybe." A slight bitterness crept into her tone.

"Easier for both of us."

Her skin was pale, like an alabaster bowl, and before he could stop himself, Jack lifted a hand and skimmed his knuckles down her cheek.

She frowned, but didn't move away. And when his thumb grazed her lips, she closed her eyes and shuddered.

"I should tell you not to do that," she said.

"Why don't you?"

She sighed. "Because it's been a very long time since anyone's touched me. And I'm well aware of how pathetic that sounds."

He didn't really understand what she meant, but he could sense her loneliness. A strange melancholy tugged at him, too, along with a rush of excitement. His heart pounded as he stared down at her. "You're beautiful," he said. "I had no idea."

She smiled a little at that. "I thought you saw me in a vision."

"Not clearly. Not like this." His gaze devoured her face—the soft. pink lips; the wide, brown eyes; the cloud of blond hair that curled about her shoulders.

She stared up at him, lips parted and waiting, and for the longest moment, he stood there trapped in her spell, enthralled by the darkest of gazes. And then a car engine sounded, and they both whirled toward the road.

"We should go," Claudia said breathlessly. "Probably not a good idea to be standing out in the open like this."

He kicked himself for the lapse. "Where are we going?" To the hospital? To the police station?

She thought about that for a moment. "Home," she said finally. "Let's just go home."

Chapter Eighteen

As it turned out, they didn't go directly home, but instead stopped at a large sporting goods and camping store in Rapid City. If they were going to do this—whatever *this* was—Claudia decided that Jack needed more suitable attire.

So they spent some time outfitting him with boots, wool socks, a parka, shirts, jeans and underwear—thermal and otherwise. The purchases took a sizeable bite out of Claudia's cash on hand and Jack protested every step of the way, but she remained adamant. No way could she allow him to go out again in such flimsy clothing. She didn't want to have to feel guilty each time she bundled up for an excursion.

Besides, she thought a little acerbically. If Jack really had come there to save her, buying him some new clothes was the least she could do to repay him. And her reasoning—she freely admitted—spoke volumes to her rapid change of heart. Jack had pretty much won her over.

Abetted by her instincts and, yes, maybe her loneliness, she was now willing to give him the benefit of the doubt. Whoever he was and wherever he'd come from didn't matter so much anymore because Claudia was no longer afraid of him.

While he changed in the dressing room, she stood at the large plate glass window and stared out at the street. Behind the row of businesses rose the Dakota Hogback, a small mountain range that divided the city in two. The mist was finally clearing and she had no trouble making out the peaks. But the day was still overcast with little chance of the sun breaking through, so if Jack's interpretation of his vision was correct, there would be no need to go back to Mount Rushmore today.

Claudia was thankful for that. She could use a little time to get used to the idea. Being on the run was one thing. Trying to save a child's life from unknown "tangos" was something else altogether.

She couldn't quite believe how quickly she'd waded into the deep end. After all, she'd known Jack for less than a day. A part of her still worried that she was being impulsive and irresponsible while another part wanted to rush headlong into *Jack and Claudia's Excellent Adventure.* She hadn't realized until he showed up just how empty her life had been for the past two years. How much she'd craved companionship, a little excitement. Now she certainly had that. In spades.

Speaking of which…

She moved closer to the window. There wasn't much

traffic this time of day, which was probably why she happened to notice the man standing across the street. He was tall, broad-shouldered and bald-headed, but what captured her interest was the way he stood so still, head tilted back, eyes closed, completely oblivious to everything and everyone around him.

He wore a long black coat, black pants, boots. He didn't look at all like he belonged in Rapid City.

Claudia's heart fluttered in alarm, although she really wasn't sure why. A lot of tourists came through the area, so that was no big deal. And unlike the man at the monument, the stranger across the street didn't seem familiar to her in the least. She'd never seen him before, or anyone who looked remotely like him. His skin, what she could see of it, had an almost ghostlike pallor, and in spite of the gray day, his bald head seemed to reflect light. He was an odd-looking man. *Very* odd. And Claudia couldn't take her eyes off him.

Her blood tingled as a little frisson of goose flesh lifted the hair at her nape. She stood rooted, staring, even though she had to fight a sudden urge to dart into the nearest hiding place. She had no idea why because the man's behavior, while peculiar, wasn't particularly threatening.

Then, as if he'd been trapped in the deepest of trances, he snapped to his senses. His head came down as his gaze swept the street like a predator searching for prey.

Without thinking, Claudia stepped back from the

glass a split second before he focused in on the window. His attention lingered, moved on, then returned. He tilted his head back again and closed his eyes briefly before moving on down the street.

"Are you ready to go?"

Claudia hadn't realized she'd been holding her breath, but now at the sound of Jack's voice behind her, she jumped as the air came swooshing out of her lungs in a painful rush. Her hand flew to her chest as if she could somehow suppress the hard knock of her heart.

Jack's voice sharpened. "What's wrong?"

"Did you see that man across the street?" She turned quickly back to the window. The bald stranger was nowhere in sight. She stepped up to the glass and glanced out. Gone. How could he have disappeared so quickly?

Claudia's imagination started to take flight, but she quickly reined it in. Obviously, he'd turned down another street or stepped into one of the businesses. There was nothing sinister about any of this.

No need to see a bogeyman around every corner just because killers are out there looking for you, she thought dryly.

"Claudia?"

She jerked around. "Yeah?"

"What man?" Jack asked in concern. "The same one you saw at the monument?"

"No, this guy was different.... I'm pretty sure I've never seen him before. It's just..." She shook her head.

"I don't know. All of a sudden, I'm seeing menacing strangers everywhere I go. Present company excepted," she tried to quip.

She glanced up at Jack, but his gaze was now fastened on the street. For a moment, she wondered if he'd caught a glimpse of the bald man, but when she looked back toward the street, she saw a dark blue car idling at the traffic light.

She spun back to Jack. His gaze was so intense, her stomach fluttered in apprehension. "What's wrong?"

He said nothing. Dropping the packages of clothing, he turned and raced out of the store. By the time Claudia overcame her shock and rushed after him, he was half a block away.

"Hey!"

At her call, he paused, his gaze still on the street. The blue car was up ahead of him and gaining speed.

"Jack?" She hurried to his side. "What's going on? Why'd you run out like that—"

He turned and grabbed her arms. "We have to follow that car."

For a moment, the overly-dramatic command didn't even compute. It was like a line out of every bad mystery movie Claudia had ever seen. "What are you talking about? What car? You mean the blue one that just passed by here? Why?"

Jack's grip tightened. "The boy's inside. I saw him in the backseat."

His agitated tone, more than his words, finally

penetrated Claudia's fog. "What? You mean the boy in your vision?"

"I saw him in the backseat of that car. We have to find him—"

"Okay, okay, but we can't catch a car on foot. We'll have to go back and get mine." When he seemed reluctant to follow her, she tugged on his arm. "Come on. If we let them get too far ahead, we could lose them."

He glanced back at the street, then nodded and they both took off running back to the SUV.

Climbing inside, Claudia started the engine and executed a U-turn in the road before flooring the accelerator. She gave a silent prayer of thanks for the sparse traffic because she drove like a madwoman. Unfortunately, the blue car was already out of sight.

"Hurry," Jack muttered.

"I'm doing my best." She flashed him a look as she navigated along the street. The scenery flew by them. "Are you sure it was the same boy?"

"Yes."

"Did you get a look at the driver?"

"Barely. I think it was a woman."

"The kidnapper?"

"I don't think so."

"Then who…" Claudia broke off. "Oh, of course, he's probably with his mother. He hasn't been taken yet. If we catch up to them…" She paused again. "Jack, what the heck are we going to tell her?"

He said nothing.

Claudia spared another glance. "I mean, we can't very well tell her the truth, can we? She'll think we're a couple of crackpots. Probably call the police on us. We could end up in jail or worse and that poor kid will be on his own. Jack?"

He was so silent, Claudia wondered if he'd gone into some kind of trance, leaving her to figure out their immediate course of action. Which she didn't like one bit because what on earth could she tell the kid's mother that would convince her of the impending danger?

This man is a pre-cog. He had a vision about your son. He's become the target of a kidnapper. Whatever you do, don't take him to Mount Rushmore.

Oh, yeah. That little spiel would go over really well.

But what else did they have on their side but the truth? Or at least, Jack's version of the truth. How else to warn the boy's mother except by coming clean with her? Of course, that was assuming she would even give them the chance—

A traffic light up ahead turned yellow, and Claudia cursed under her breath as she pressed the gas pedal even harder. *Don't turn red,* she silently pleaded as the vehicle approached the intersection. They were losing ground with every second that ticked by. The blue car was nowhere in sight, and for all Claudia knew, it had already turned off somewhere. In which case, they might never be able to find it.

"You didn't happen to get the license-plate number, did you?" she asked Jack.

More silence.

They entered the intersection just as the light changed and Claudia cringed as she glanced both ways down the street. Thankfully, no traffic was coming from either direction and they made it through without so much as a close call. At least for the moment, luck was on their side—

The blast of a siren sounded behind her and when she looked in the rearview mirror, she saw the flashing rotation of police lights.

"Great. Just great." She glanced over at Jack. The siren had brought him out of his trance and he turned to look out the back window. "I have to pull over. I can't outrun the police." A high-speed chase through the streets of Rapid City would not only be stupid and potentially dangerous, but also a sure-fire way to expose her cover. She could see her picture now flashed across every news broadcast in the state. If Dr. Lasher's killer wasn't already on her trail, he soon would be.

"Go ahead and pull over," Jack said.

She slowed the car and eased to the shoulder. "Okay, we have to think fast here. How should we handle this? Do we tell them about the boy?"

"They'd never believe us."

"I know, but—" She glanced in the rearview mirror. The officer was already out of the patrol car and heading toward them. "Jack? Help me out here. I need to know what to tell them—"

But it was too late. The officer was already rapping

on the glass and Claudia had no choice but to roll down the window. Reaching in her bag, she pulled out her driver's license and proof of insurance, then handed everything to the officer.

He glanced at the photo I.D., looked at her then scrutinized the insurance paperwork. "Are you aware that you ran a red light back there, Miss?"

"It was yellow when I entered the intersection."

"No, it wasn't. It was clearly red."

Claudia cleared her throat. "If you're sure, then I suppose I have to take your word for it."

"You were also going seventeen miles over the posted speed limit. Where's the fire?"

She glanced at Jack who stared back at her with a tiny shrug. Obviously, dealing with the police was a bit out of his wheelhouse, so Claudia had to think fast. How much did she dare tell the officer? Too much, and he'd think they were nutcases, maybe even take them into custody. Obviously, this had to be handled carefully.

And all of a sudden Claudia had an idea. She remembered something Jack had told her the night before about changing her destiny.

She glanced up at the officer and allowed a note of wary excitement to creep into her voice. "Officer, you know the boy who was kidnapped a few weeks ago on a camping trip with his parents?"

He gave her a curious onceover. "You mean the Lafferty kid?"

Claudia swallowed. "Yes. His picture has been all over the news. This is going to sound crazy, but…I thought I saw him in a car that was just ahead of us. A blue sedan. He was in the backseat. I was trying to catch up to the car so that we could get a better look."

Beside her Jack was very still, but she could sense his tension, his scrutiny.

He must be wondering what the hell I'm doing.

She tried to communicate via thought transference. *Trust me. I know what I'm doing. There's a method to my madness.*

The officer was still staring down at her. Was it her imagination, or was that a suspicious glint in his eyes. "Did you get a license-plate number?"

"Unfortunately, I couldn't make it out. By the time I figured out why the kid looked so familiar, they were already too far ahead of us. Look…" She gave him a pleading glance. "I don't know if it was the same boy. All I know for certain is that if I didn't check it out and it *was* him, I'd never forgive myself. So can you please…I don't know…put out an APB or whatever it is that you do?"

The officer's gaze went to Jack. "What about you? You see the boy?"

Jack shrugged. "Just barely a glance. But it could have been him."

"What about the make and model of the car?"

"It looked fairly new," Claudia said. "But that's about all I can tell you. It went by pretty fast. A blue sedan."

He nodded to Jack. "Did you get a better look at the car?"

"Like she said, it was a blue sedan."

"You don't know the make?"

Jack lifted one shoulder. "No, sorry. If the car is still on this road, it shouldn't be hard to find. But time could be of the essence."

The officer remained skeptical. "Just wait right here for a minute."

He went back to his car, and through the rearview mirror, Claudia saw him get on his radio. He was gone for only a couple of minutes before he sauntered back up to her window.

"I'm going to let you off with a warning this time," he said gruffly. "But speeding and running a traffic light, no matter the reason, are serious offenses."

"I understand. And thank you, officer. But what about the boy?" Claudia asked anxiously.

"We'll handle it from here." He slapped a hand on the roof, dismissing them. "Take it easy."

"Yeah, we will," Claudia said as she put away her driver's license and proof of insurance.

She waited until the patrol car pulled out around them and disappeared down the street before glancing at Jack. "I know, I know, what on earth was I thinking?"

"Why did you lie about the boy?"

"Because I couldn't tell him the truth, could I? That the boy you saw in the backseat will be kidnapped at Mount Rushmore. Like you said, he'd never have believed us. But now if the police find the blue car, pull the driver over and check out our story, it could alter the course of events. Change the kid's destiny or something." She shrugged helplessly, realizing how crazy her rationalization sounded. "It seemed like a good idea at the time, and it was all I could think to do."

"You did fine."

His quiet words were hardly reassuring. "But you don't think it'll change anything, do you?"

"No," he said grimly. "The boy's destiny is still in our hands."

"I was afraid you were going to say that." Claudia glanced down at her palms. They were sweating and she was shaking all over. God help her, she was not cut out for this.

God help that poor child, too.

Chapter Nineteen

When they got home that afternoon, Claudia decided she needed to spend some time working. She had several projects due to go live in a matter of days and there were always updates that needed to be done.

Just because some weird pre-cog had a vision of my impending death is no reason to let myself fall behind. Ha-ha.

Smiling wryly to herself, she sat down at her computer and sorted through her e-mail.

Jack, all bundled up in his new parka, boots and gloves went outside to give her some space. At least, that was the excuse he gave her, but Claudia suspected there was more to it than that. She remembered what he'd said at the monument. Since they didn't know the enemy, they could at least know the terrain.

Claudia tried to immerse herself in her work, but after a few minutes, she got up, stretched and drifted over to the window to look out. Jack was nowhere in sight, and she resisted the urge to go and search for him.

Instead, she made herself go back to the desk, plant her butt in front of the computer and prioritize the updates.

It took some effort, but she finally managed to lose herself in the work, so much so that hours went by without her knowing. When she finally reached a stopping point, she was surprised to look up and find the cabin had grown quite gloomy. The light was fading rapidly and a chill had settled over the room.

And Jack was still not back.

After saving her work, Claudia got up and turned on some lights and lit a fire. Then after checking out the window, she went into the kitchen to start dinner.

By this time, Jack had been gone for hours, but Claudia told herself she wouldn't worry about him. Nor would she dwell on what he might be doing out there. He was a big boy, he could take care of himself.

Besides, if the transformation she'd witnessed at the monument was any indication, he was in his element outside. He'd be okay. Claudia wasn't concerned. Not in the least.

Still, the window drew her time and again as she prepared a simple pasta dish and made a salad. She set the table, opened a bottle of wine, lit some candles and dimmed the lights. With a crackling fire in the hearth, the cabin was already warm and cozy. One might even say romantic.

What do you think you're doing? a little voice demanded as she stood back and examined her handiwork. Candles, wine, a toasty fire. *How much more obvious can you be?*

Loneliness was one thing, but this was just…sad. And reeked of desperation.

Come on, C.J. You're better than this.

"Okay, you win," she muttered as she leaned over to blow out the candles.

A knock sounded on the door and she spun. Then she let out a relieved breath. It was probably just Jack. She'd locked the door behind him and he didn't have a key.

Still, Claudia wasn't taking any chances. Grabbing the revolver from her desk, she slipped it in her pocket and kept her hand on the grip as she moved to the door.

"Who is it?"

"Jack."

She slipped the gun in her pocket as she slid back the bolt. When she opened the door, a blast of frigid air followed Jack inside. The candle flames danced wildly, casting huge shadows on the walls and ceiling, and a log shifted in the fireplace, causing her to jump. Suddenly, the room didn't look so cozy anymore. It was strange, but with Jack's return, a host of insecurities and fears invaded Claudia's house.

"You've sure been gone a long time." She winced at the note of accusation in her voice.

He shrugged out of his coat and hung it on a hook by the door. "I went for walk."

"That was a mighty long walk," Claudia said.

"Yes." He went over to the fireplace to warm his hands.

She trailed along behind him. "You were out there

reconnoitering, weren't you? Familiarizing yourself with the terrain around my cabin."

He didn't bother to deny it.

"Why?" Claudia asked nervously. "Do you think we're in danger here?"

"I think we're in danger everywhere," he said, and the look he gave her sent a deep shiver down Claudia's spine. "We have to be prepared."

"For what?"

His silence spoke volumes.

Claudia drew a breath and released it. "Okay, this is probably something we need to talk about, but right now dinner is ready and I just want to have a quiet meal. Are you hungry?"

"Yes."

"All right, get washed up and we'll eat."

While he disappeared into the bathroom, Claudia contemplated blowing out the candles and getting rid of the wine. A little romance no longer seemed like such a good idea. But Jack had already seen the table, so what would be the point?

Besides, this was nothing out of the ordinary for her. She frequently lit candles and had wine with dinner. Okay, she frequently had wine with dinner. The candles not so much, but still…

Stop being so defensive, she chided herself. A candlelit dinner was no big deal. It didn't have to lead to anything. Besides, Jack's preparations for whatever might be coming their way had put a damper on the whole evening. Claudia wanted to relax, but that didn't seem too likely at the moment. Not without some deep breaths and a whole lot of that wine.

"It's nice in here."

She whirled. She hadn't heard Jack come in. Even in boots, he moved quietly. He stood only a few feet from her, candlelight flickering over his face. And her mind went instantly to the previous night and the way the light had played over every inch of his body.

Her breath quickened as their gazes clung. She'd been trying to put that image out of her head all day and mostly she'd succeeded because she'd had other things to worry about. But now with Jack so close, with the attraction she'd already admitted to sizzling between them, a whole lot of memories came pouring back. The breadth of his shoulders, the depth of his bare chest. All those sinewy muscles.

She swallowed and looked away. "Have a seat."

"Can't I help?"

"It's all ready. Here." She handed him the bottle of wine. "You can pour."

He went to the table and filled the wineglasses. Claudia brought over the pasta and salad and they helped themselves. Once again she noticed the restrained way he ate, as if having to hold himself back from devouring the whole plate. And the way he tentatively sipped the wine, as if wary of the taste.

"What's the matter?" she asked. "Don't you like wine?"

He took another sip. "It's good."

His hesitation over the wine was strange. It was like he'd never had it before and Claudia wondered again at his background. He'd seemed so lost, the night before. Almost childlike in his naiveté. But over the course of the day, everything about his persona, including his word choices, had grown increasingly more sophisticated and complex. But there was still something very sheltered about him, as if he didn't quite fit in the real world.

Preoccupied by her thoughts, Claudia only nibbled on her food, but she had no problem at all in polishing off her first glass of wine. She poured another glass and brought it to her mouth, watching him over the rim.

His head was slightly bowed so that she couldn't see his eyes. That was a very good thing because his deep blue gaze was killer.

The circumstances of her exile had made her rightfully wary and sometimes overly cautious, but she was still so young and life was passing her by so fast she could barely stand to think about it. And yet for all the trouble he'd brought into her life, she felt herself coming back to life in Jack's company.

They were both so quiet tonight, and she was afraid the prolonged silence would soon become awkward so she tried to draw him out.

"I've been thinking about what happened earlier," she said. "I'm wondering if the cops were able to track down that blue car. Or if they even tried to. I suppose I could call the police department, but I doubt they'd tell me anything.

His head came up and he looked at her with those dark and mysterious eyes. "I don't think it matters if they found the car or not. Nothing has changed."

"How do you know?"

"I'd know."

She picked up her wineglass. "But what about the butterfly effect? One tiny alteration and *voilà!* The whole course of history is changed."

"You're assuming that today was never meant to happen. We were never supposed to see that car, get stopped by the police." He shrugged. "Nothing's changed."

Claudia sat back in her chair and stared at him in silence.

"The boy will be taken at the monument," Jack said. "That's where we have to stop them."

"Them."

Maybe one, maybe many.

Claudia gulped her wine. "It would be helpful if we had a little more to go on. You haven't remembered anything?"

He glanced back down at his plate, but not before Claudia had seen a look of revulsion flash across his features. He picked up his wineglass and drank deeply. His hand on the stem was rock steady, but she could tell that he was troubled.

"You did remember something, didn't you?"

He drained the wine and she poured him some more.

"Tell me," she coaxed softly.

"I remember looking through metal bars," he said finally. "I remember being locked up."

The nerves in Claudia's stomach clenched painfully. "You mean like…prison?"

"Not the kind of prison you mean. We didn't do anything wrong."

"Then…where were you?"

He still didn't look at her. "In a place called the Facility."

"That was the name of it, the Facility?"

"That's the only thing I ever knew it by."

"What kind of place is it?"

"A very bad place." An edge of anger crept into his voice, but he still didn't look up.

"Where is this place?" Claudia asked.

"I don't know."

"What were you doing there?"

He lifted a hand to his neck. Again, she saw a look of loathing in his eyes, along with a flare of rage. "I think we were part of an experiment."

A tiny bomb exploded in the room. Claudia sucked in her breath. Part of an experiment? *Dear God…*

She waited for an explanation, but he said nothing else, just picked up his glass and drained it a second time.

Claudia felt she should say something, reassure him somehow. But she was completely and utterly out of her depth here.

"You were…experimented on," she managed. "How?"

"The needles."

Her gaze went to the bruises on his neck. "Yeah, I got that. But…what kind of experiments? Who performed them? And why?"

"Our abilities were being maximized to the fullest," he said.

"What kind of abilities?"

"Precognition, telepathy, telekinesis. I don't know what else."

"Telepathy?" She leaned forward and put her hand on his arm. She almost expected him to jerk away, but he didn't. For some reason, that made her very happy. "Then you really were in communication with someone earlier."

"Someone was in communication with *me.* I'm not a telepath."

"Meaning you can receive but not transmit?" When Claudia thought of the voice inside her head the night before, her scalp actually tingled. "Do you think it's someone at the Facility?"

His gaze shot to hers. "I hope not."

Her hand was still on his arm. She removed it and clasped her fingers in her lap. "For what it's worth, I don't think whoever it was means either of us any harm. The impression I got—" She stopped, searching for the right way to describe the sensation.

"The thought transference," he said.

She thought about that for a moment and nodded. "Yes. That's probably the best way to describe it. The feeling I had was one of concern. For you, actually. The impression I got was: *help him.*"

Jack frowned. "*Help him,*" he murmured.

"It was while you were sleeping. I was standing at the bedroom door. I distinctly had the feeling that this person—this entity—wanted me to help you." She paused. "Do you have any idea who it could have been?"

"No."

"Well, then, let me ask you something else. If you came here to save me…if this is all preordained or even somehow arranged…where does that boy fit into all this? How is his kidnapping part of the equation? Or is that just some weird coincidence?"

"It's not a coincidence." He held her gaze for a moment, then glanced away. "The boy's abduction is tied to the Facility."

Claudia frowned. "Connected how? You mean that's where the kidnappers will take him?"

"It's where they take all of them."

Claudia's mind flashed to the picture of the missing child she'd seen online, and she gasped as the horror of his words swept over her. "Are you saying they take them there…to be experimented on? That's why these children are disappearing? Someone is using them as human guinea pigs?"

"Yes."

A cold chill pierced her spine, and she suddenly felt sick to her stomach. "What do they do with them?"

"They maximize their abilities to the fullest."

"And when they're finished?" she whispered.

"They're never finished."

She put a hand to her mouth. "Are you saying they keep them in this place forever?"

"They can't let them go. To allow them out of the Facility would be too risky."

"Oh, my God." Even after all her work with Dr. Lasher, Claudia could hardly comprehend such a thing. Children held prisoner for years? Experimented on like lab rats? It was too horrendous to contemplate and yet she could tell from Jack's eyes that it was true. It was all true.

"This is like something..." She strove for a reference that he could comprehend. "It's like something from the *Twilight Zone*."

"Imagine if you will," he said, in an uncanny mimicry of Rod Serling's voice.

That freaked her out, and she got up and began clearing the table. This time she allowed Jack to help her. They worked in silence, and when they were finished with the dishes, they settled down in front of the fire with a fresh bottle of wine.

Claudia wasn't normally that much of a drinker, but tonight she needed a little extra fortification. After what Jack had just told her...she could still barely comprehend such a thing. No wonder he was willing to risk so much to save that boy. Suddenly, she had a whole new perspective on his mission.

Leaning back against the sofa, she studied Jack's profile as he watched the flames. She tried to imagine what he'd been through at the Facility, but there was no way she could ever know. Maybe it was a good thing he couldn't remember.

I don't like memories.

She set her wine aside and hugged her knees. She couldn't seem to tear her gaze away from him. Such a complicated man. There was always something new to discover, some new mystery to unravel. He was endlessly fascinating.

He turned and caught her staring, but she didn't look away. Instead, she lifted her glass and gazed at him over the rim.

"Tell me more about your work in Chicago," he said.

The request caught her off guard because her thoughts had been a million miles away from her old life in the Windy City. For the first time in two years, she really didn't miss that life.

"There's not much more I can tell you without getting into a lot of technical stuff. Basically, my job was to analyze the number sequences generated by the REGs."

"Random Event Generators."

"That's right. They're basically small computers that generate an endless stream of ones and zeros. The law of randomness would dictate that the number of each would be fairly uniform, but outside forces can skew the sequences, creating spikes and anomalies. For example, if you put someone in a room with an REG, their thoughts can actually influence the number sequence. So researchers and scientists began studying the correlation between large fluctuations to world events. And in some cases, the spikes and anomalies were observed before the event happened. That's where Dr. Lasher came in. He believed the REGs could be interfaced with a human pre-cog so that catastrophic events could be pinpointed and in some cases prevented before they occurred."

Claudia paused to see if Jack's eyes had glazed over yet, but to her surprise, he seemed to be following along without any difficulty. So strange. Here was a man who had expressed unfamiliarity with chamomile tea and wine, and yet was unfazed by her rather convoluted description of a random event generator.

"Shall I go on?"

He nodded.

"After Dr. Lasher left the Global Consciousness Project, he needed backing for his own private research. And that's when he got in over his head. He contacted a colleague he'd worked with in the past who was involved in some of the same kind of research. I never met or even knew the man's name, which looking back, probably should have set off some alarm bells for me. All I ever knew was that he was well-connected and well-financed by an international conglomerate of businessmen. And I suspect there may have been some high-level government officials who were also looking to exploit the findings. When Dr. Lasher found out what they were up to, he refused to cooperate. Or at least, that's what I think. He didn't confide in me, but it's not hard to figure out what happened. He threatened to go public with their intent and so they had to kill him."

Jack's eyes tracked her as she reached for her wine. "And then they came after you."

She nodded. "I saw the killer. Briefly, but I did see him. That alone would have made me a target, but they also may think that I know more about Dr. Lasher's colleague and their organization than I actually do. Like I said, he never confided in me about any of this, and looking back, I think that's because he was trying to protect me. But they wouldn't know that. To them, I'm just a loose end."

"What were you working on when Dr. Lasher was killed?"

"Me specifically? I analyzed the spikes and anomalies created by the pre-cog and tried to correlate them to real-time and future events. You know," she said slowly, "it's funny you should ask me about that because something strange happened during those last few days before Dr. Lasher died. He'd been muttering these vague warnings for quite some time, but I never really understood what he meant. I guess I just thought he was stressed and getting a little senile. But then the number sequences on the graphs began to get really screwy. I'd never seen anything like it. It was almost as if the pre-cog was using the REG to communicate with me." She shivered. "To warn me that I was in danger."

"He was."

The wineglass slipped from her fingers, but Jack's hand had already shot out to catch it. He set the glass aside without spilling a drop.

Claudia couldn't breathe, and the tension inside her chest became almost unbearable. "How do you know the pre-cog was trying to warn me?"

His gaze deepened but he said nothing.

She put a hand to her throat. "Are you saying…it was you?"

More silence.

"There's a reason why I ended up here, isn't there?" she whispered. Something had compelled her to drive north by northwest the night she fled Chicago. Something had guided her to this cabin where she had been waiting for two long years. "There's a reason why you're here now."

She reached out, touched his cheek tentatively with her fingertips. When he didn't resist, she cupped his face in her hands and stroked a finger across one eyebrow, down his nose, over his lips.

"You know me," he said.

Yes, she did know him and she understood why now. Call it destiny or whatever, but the notion that this was all meant to be both frightened and excited her even as she closed her eyes and accepted it.

Never one to shy away from her natural urges, Claudia moved in closer and brought her lips to his, lightly, tenderly. No pressure or expectations. Just an experimental brush.

Her heart started to beat so fast she could scarcely breathe. She pulled away, startled by her reaction.

"I liked that," he said and ran his fingers through her hair. He lifted a strand to his nose and inhaled deeply. "Flowers."

"I'm not sure…if we should be doing this," she said, completely taken aback by her response to him.

"We aren't doing anything."

"Not yet, we're not." She gave into the temptation once again and ran her hand across his shoulder, down his arm, entangling her fingers with his.

He stared down at their interlocked hands for the longest time. Then his gaze lifted and Claudia caught her breath. His eyes…so blue, so deep.

Those eyes killed her every time.

She moved in again, this time wrapping her arms around his neck, drawing her to him as she placed her mouth on his. He didn't resist, nor did he respond. For maybe a half second. Then his lips opened and Claudia intensified the kiss. She pressed harder, searched deeper, and then suddenly their roles reversed as he plowed his fingers through her hair. He drew away, murmured something she didn't understand, and then he kissed her again.

It seemed to go on forever and yet it was over in the space of a heartbeat. Jack wrenched himself free, stared at her for a moment then slid away from her.

"What's wrong?" she whispered.

Pulling his knees to his chest, he sat with his fingertips pressed tightly to his temples as he rocked back and forth.

Claudia was instantly beside him. "Jack, are you okay?"

His face had gone pale. "I can hear him screaming again."

"Who?"

"I don't know. I can't get out. The cage is locked..."

Cage? *Dear God.*

She put a hand on his shoulder but he flinched away. Helpless to know what to do, she sat back on her heels and watched him.

"It's all my fault," he said in anguish. "I caused this."

"What did you cause?"

"The escape. It was my idea. But when they caught us, he took the blame."

"Who took the blame?"

It was as if he didn't even hear her. "We'll see how you like it at the Facility," he said in a strange voice. "No one has ever escaped from there."

"Jack." Tentatively, she placed her hand on his arm. This time he didn't move away. "Your memory is coming back, isn't it?"

He groaned.

"Is there anything I can do?"

He dug his fingertips into his temples. "Make them stop."

"I wish I could." She squeezed his arm in reassurance. "Do you want to talk about it?"

He drew himself up even tighter and shivered. "I'm cold."

She fetched a blanket off the bed and wrapped it around his shoulders. Then she put her arms around him and drew him close.

After a while, he slid down to the floor and laid his head in her lap. She stroked his hair and he let her. She hummed softly and he closed his eyes.

They stayed that way for a long time, hours and hours, until the fire died down and the cold light of dawn crept into the room.

Chapter Twenty

Just after daybreak, Claudia, eased away from Jack and stretched her cramped muscles. Then she padded off to the bedroom, climbed into bed and promptly fell asleep. She woke up a few hours later to another gray day. From the window she could see the distant hills peeping through the haze.

No sunlight meant no kidnapping.

It was an odd thought with which to start the day, but Claudia's life hadn't been normal for a very long time.

She lay for a moment, luxuriating in the warmth of the blankets and wishing she could just tuck her head under and stay for a while. But it was already mid-morning and she needed to get a start on the day. She had things to do, and as Jack was fond of saying, time was of the essence.

Throwing off the covers, she rose. Still sleepy-eyed, she crossed the room and poked her head out the door. The fire had died out and the room was chilly. Empty.

She stepped through the door and glanced around. The blanket from the night before was neatly folded on the end of the sofa, but Jack was nowhere to be seen.

"Jack?"

He was gone, but Claudia didn't panic, nor did she bother looking for him out the window. She had a feeling she knew where he was. He'd probably headed out first thing to have another look around the cabin. To reconnoiter the terrain.

To be honest, she wasn't sure how she felt about that. She supposed his diligence should have reassured her, but his attention to such matters kept her a little unnerved because it hammered home his assertion that she was in danger. That the only way he could save her was to change her destiny.

Well, he'd already done that, hadn't he? Just by showing up.

With a tingling sense of new discovery, Claudia thought about the kiss they'd shared the night before, and her fingertips crept to her lips.

There had been something both a little chaste and completely erotic about his response, and she couldn't help remembering what he'd told her about the Facility. The kidnapped boys were taken there and held indefinitely for experimentation. So how long had he been there? Since childhood?

That would explain some of his stranger reactions to commonplace things, such as the taste of chamomile tea and the wine. And yet he wasn't wholly naive because he seemed pretty familiar with her computer, the television, even the police yesterday.

He was an enigma in every sense of the word, and Claudia wondered if she would ever know much more about him than she did at that moment. Was that enough?

She found herself at the window after all, although she wasn't really looking for Jack. Instead she watched the haze lift over the mountains, as though some great veil had been stripped away. The sun didn't come out, but the day lightened and a mild breeze stirred the wind chimes on her front porch.

A leaf hung suspended in a draft for a split second before winnowing down to the ground. Then the wind died away and all was calm.

Turning away from the window, Claudia padded back to the bedroom and grabbing some clothes, headed for the bathroom. Since she had the cabin to herself, she used the opportunity to take a leisurely shower and wash her hair. By the time she came out a little while later, Jack had returned and was planted in front of the television watching an episode of *Charlie's Angels.*

"Good morning."

He responded with a murmur, but he seemed barely aware of her presence. He didn't even bother to glance up as she moved around him to the kitchen. She tried not to take it personally. Maybe he was feeling a little awkward about the night before. More likely, though, he was just absorbed in the program, and Claudia freely acknowledged that she was no match for Farrah, Jaclyn and Kate. But then, who was?

As she cracked eggs for an omelet, her gaze kept straying to the living room. Jack had donned some of his new clothes—jeans, boots and a long sleeve gray T-shirt that she imagined would do incredible things for his eyes, if she could see them. She liked to think her pale green sweater did great things for her coloring, too, but for all Jack's interest, she may as well have been wearing a paper bag over her head.

But she couldn't help smiling. His weird fascination for old TV shows was both ridiculous and utterly endearing. And yet another intriguing piece of the Jack puzzle.

She turned from the stove and there he was, stealthy as always.

Luckily, nothing was in her hand or she most certainly would have dropped it. But, of course, he would have anticipated her clumsiness and come to her rescue yet again.

"I wish you'd stop doing that! My nerves can't take it! If I don't have a heart attack while you're here, it'll be a miracle."

He didn't smile. As always, he seemed to take everything she said very seriously. "I'm sorry. I came to see if I could help."

"No, everything's ready." She tried to calm her stomach flutters, but when she looked up at him, her heart skidded against her ribcage.

Oh, boy, had she ever been right. The gray T-shirt did amazing things to his eyes. Made them look deeper, darker, bluer. And so magnetic she almost felt a physical pull.

Turning abruptly, she divided the omelet and stacked each plate with toast and orange slices. "Here," she said. "You can take these to the table. I'll bring the coffee and juice."

When they were seated, she gave him a tentative glance as she unfolded her napkin. His head was bowed, and as with every meal, he seemed to concentrate intently on his food, which made Claudia wonder again about his incarceration at the Facility and how he'd been treated there.

I can hear him screaming again.

I can't get out. The cage is locked...

She took a fortifying sip of her juice. *Dear God, what the poor guy must have been through...*

Her eyes slid to him again and this time he was staring back at her. His focus was so direct, so intent, she felt her nerve endings tighten like vibrating piano wire. She held his gaze for as long as she dared, then glanced away.

"Tell me more about your life in Chicago," he said.

"I thought we covered that last night." Amazing how normal her voice sounded when her insides were doing all kinds of alarming things, like quivering and fluttering and flip-flopping all over the place.

"You told me about your job. I'd like to hear about other things."

She looked up with a frown. "What, you mean my personal life?"

He shoved his plate aside, folded his arms on the table and leaned in. His single-minded focus was still unsettling.

Claudia dabbed her mouth with the corner of her napkin. "What do you want to know?"

If possible, his eyes grew even more intense. "Did you kiss a lot of men there?"

She lifted a brow in admonishment. "That's not something you should ever ask a woman."

He looked nonplussed. "Why? There's nothing wrong with kissing is there?"

"No, not at all. It's the 'a lot of men' part that some might find objectionable," she said dryly, then shrugged. "But to answer your question, not really. Some, but not a lot. At least by my definition."

"What about sex?"

She just stared at him for a moment. "Uh, what about it?"

"Did you have sex with some of those men?"

If he hadn't looked and sounded so completely non-judgmental, Claudia might have been tempted to slap his face. However, physical violence was never her first choice, and besides, he just seemed so darned innocent and genuinely curious, she couldn't muster up enough outrage to hold it against him. "Let me just turn that question around on you," she said. "What about you?"

"I don't remember."

"You don't remember having sex? Well, lucky for you it's like riding a bicycle. You never forget how. Unless..." A thought struck her. Dumbfounded her. "You've never...uh..." She made an involuntary gesture with her finger. "You know."

She almost expected him to sputter an indignant denial or turn away in embarrassment, but instead his gaze remained steadfast and completely unfazed. "I can't remember."

Wow. Just...wow.

This was not something Claudia had let herself contemplate. But she supposed it made sense, if he'd been held against his will since childhood.

A part of her really wanted to question him further, but mostly, she thought it a subject best left alone for the moment. She wasn't ready for a conversation that personal, no matter how rampant her curiosity.

Hopping up from the table, she started grabbing dishes. "We can talk more about this later if you want. Right now, I have to get to work. I'll just clear the table..."

"Here, let me do that."

Their hands brushed when they reached for the same glass, and Claudia drew back, startled. Such a small, insignificant touch, and yet her skin still tingled from the contact. "Okay, we can both do it," she said breathlessly.

Their gazes met again, he smiled slowly and Claudia felt the bottom drop out of her world. She tried not to stare, but it was like a moth to a flame.

Virgin or not, he had her wound up in knots. This new persona of his exuded mystery and confidence and all kinds of crazy sex appeal.

Good thing he's been locked up in a cage all these years, she thought.

A smile like that could spontaneously impregnate every adult female within a ten-mile radius.

AFTER BREAKFAST, CLAUDIA set Jack up with her laptop, showed him how to use Google and then settled in at her desk to get some work done.

Every now and then, though, she would glance over to see what he was doing. As with everything, he seemed wholly absorbed in the task at hand, surfing from one site to another, apparently soaking up information like the proverbial sponge.

She could watch him for hours.

But her hopeless fascination wouldn't pay the bills so she forced herself to concentrate on her own task at hand. When she looked up again a little while later, Jack was still sitting with the computer on his lap, staring at an image on the screen. Claudia thought nothing of it at first and went back to her own work. Then her gaze returned to Jack. He remained focused on that image. And he wasn't moving. His utter stillness was eerie and unsettling.

She got up from the desk and walked to the couch to stare at the screen over his shoulder. It was a strange eight-sided star, a design Claudia had never seen before. And the image had been animated in such a way that the center of the star appeared to pulse against the black background.

Claudia stood mesmerized by the movement. “What is that?”

Nothing but silence.

An uneasy chill skittered up her spine. She tore her gaze from the image and moved around to perch on the arm of the sofa. “Jack?”

He didn’t answer, didn’t move, didn’t so much as blink. He appeared completely entranced by the image.

She snapped her fingers near his face and he didn’t even notice.

It’s like he’s in a trance or something.

Her hands were dry and icy as she rubbed them along her jeans.

What if he’s hypnotized?

How was she supposed to bring him out of it? What if she said or did the wrong thing? What if she sent him into an even deeper stupor?

“Jack?” She spoke in barely a whisper. “Can you hear me?”

Slowly, his gaze lifted from the screen. He must have heard her, and yet his eyes looked distant, vacant.

Like no one’s at home.

Her heart sped until it was slamming against her chest in painful little strokes. “Jack?”

He blinked twice.

Oh, thank God, Claudia thought in relief. Maybe he was coming out of it on his own. "Are you okay?"

Another blink, then he moistened his lips. "Yes. No." He drew a shuddering breath. "I remember now."

She could feel her pulse all the way down to her fingertips. "What do you remember?"

Another breath. He glanced back at the star and seemed to lose himself in the undulation for a moment. Then he looked up and his eyes were filled with a sort of hopeless dread that was terrible to witness.

"Everything," he said. "I remember…everything."

Chapter Twenty-One

Jack stood shivering in the cold. He'd left Claudia and all her questions behind in the cabin because he needed some time to process the storm of memories flooding through him. He knew who he was now. He knew where he had come from, where he had been, what he was supposed to be. He also knew why the "voice" calling to him inside his head the day before had seemed so familiar. It was his twin brother, Jared.

He lifted his head to the sky and closed his eyes as he tried to open his mind. *Where are you? Where are you?*

Nothing came through. No sound at all but the wind in the trees, the flap of a hawk's wing, the trickle of the creek behind Claudia's house.

And the memory of those screams.

He put his hands to his temples and pressed. *Where are you? Where are you?*

"Jack?"

He whirled. Claudia had come up behind him, all

bundled up in her parka. She handed him his coat and gloves. "I thought you might be cold."

"Thanks." He took the garments and drew them on.

"Do you need anything?" she asked hesitantly. Her eyes looked very dark and very worried. He wanted to put her at ease, but he didn't know how he was supposed to do that when his own mind was in such torment.

"I'm okay," he said.

She nodded. "I'll be inside if you change your mind and want to talk or something." She turned and started toward the cabin.

"Claudia?"

"Yes?"

When he didn't say anything, she waited. Her expression seemed guarded but also a little hopeful, he thought. Or maybe that was just wishful thinking because at the moment, he desperately needed for someone to care.

"Don't go."

Myriad emotions flashed across her face. Hope. Fear. Worry. Relief. "Are you sure? Because I understand if you need some time alone."

"I need—" He wanted to say "you," but he wasn't sure that was appropriate, considering. After all, what did he have to offer a woman like Claudia except protection? He couldn't give her love, long-term companionship. Those things were not for someone like him.

"What do you need?" she asked softly.

He gave a little shrug. "Maybe we could go for a walk or something."

She lifted a brow in surprise. "Walk? Sure, why not. I like to walk."

Although Jack had made it a point to familiarize himself with the surrounding terrain, he let Claudia take the lead. He followed her around to the back of the cabin where a narrow trail led into the woods.

They walked single file and after a while, he began to relax. The spell of the forest was potent. Everything was so still and silent, and the air smelled of pine needles and the earthy scent of moss and lichen that clung to the bark of the trees and the northern side of the rocks. Clean smells. Comforting smells.

They were in no particular hurry, but Claudia had struck a fairly brisk pace. She was in good shape. Her legs worked like pistons as her arms swung beside her. He admired that about her. He admired everything about her.

After a bit, she veered off the path and they began a gentle climb to a craggy summit that overlooked a purple valley ringed by thick, blackish conifers.

The air was fresh and cold, and for Jack, cleansing. There, in nature's cathedral, the cramped gloom of a ten-foot by ten-foot cage seemed more like a nightmare than an actual memory.

Claudia perched on a flat boulder and after a moment, Jack sat down beside her. He knew she was curious about what he had remembered, but she was courteous enough not to press. He appreciated that.

The memories were still too fresh, and there were so many things running through his head that he still didn't understand.

The one question he couldn't get away from, though, was the fate of his brother.

Where are you? Where are you?

He looked up at the sky, searched the mountains and the valley.

Where are you?

Beside him, Claudia began to talk, her breath frosting on the cold air. "When I was a little girl, my father used to take me to Wisconsin on these camping trips. I wasn't really the outdoorsy type, not back then, but I never could say no because those trips meant so much to him." She halted as she looked up at the mountains. "He grew up in a small town and I don't think he ever felt at home in Chicago. He probably wouldn't have lasted more than a few months if he hadn't met my mother." She gave a little laugh. "She was really something."

"I can imagine," he murmured, watching her.

She smiled at that. "Actually, I look more like my dad. He and my mother were complete opposites. She was a city girl through and through. What we call high maintenance these days. She loved to shop, get her nails done, buy all the latest fashions and cosmetics. My dad was all about the basics. And yet they were so crazy about each other. I remember how they used to hold hands when we watched movies together and how they would look at each other across the dinner table. It was like they shared this amazing secret. I always wondered what that would be like."

"You've never…been in love?"

She shook her head. "No, not even close. But I guess there are some advantages to going it alone. You can't lose what you never had. My poor mother was devastated when my dad died."

"How old were you?"

"Eleven. She was never the same. She was a beautiful woman and she had plenty of admirers over the years, but she never remarried. She just couldn't get over my dad. She used to tell me that I looked just like him, and I sometimes wonder now how she was able to bear such a constant reminder."

"Maybe you reminded her of what she loved most about him. Maybe it was a comfort."

Her smile was wan. "I'd like to think so."

"Where is she now?"

"She died during my freshman year of college. Breast cancer. I never even knew she was sick until it was too far gone. But at least we got to say good-bye and that's more than some people get." She bent and plucked a brown leaf from the damp ground and gently traced the points with her fingertip.

Jack felt a tug of sorrow as he watched her. He wasn't sure if the sadness was for her or for him. "I'm sorry about your parents."

She released the leaf and watched it drift back down

to the ground. "At least I have my memories. That's a good thing."

He said nothing to that.

She turned on the boulder to face him. "But your memories aren't so good, are they, Jack?"

"No."

"You don't have to tell me anything if you don't want to. But if and when you do need to talk, I'm here."

He watched a bird swoop down toward the treetops. "I wouldn't even know where to start."

"Tell about that website you found earlier. You were staring so intently at that star. It was almost as if you were in a trance. Had you seen it before?"

A thrill of unease raced up his spine. "I don't know."

"Do you remember how you found it?"

He thought about that for a moment, then shook his head.

"Did you use Google? What did you type in the search engine?"

"I don't remember."

"Well, don't worry about it. I can search the history. What I'm more curious about now is the affect it seemed to have on you." Her eyes narrowed as she studied him. "I'm wondering if that star somehow triggered your memory. Maybe you were subconsciously drawn to that website for a reason, and the image of the star worked like a post-hypnotic suggestion." She grew more and more excited as she continued. "Maybe someone out there is trying to reach out to you."

Or find me, Jack thought.

"It's the only thing that makes sense," Claudia insisted. "Think about it. You barely know how to use the computer. I had to show you how to use Google, and yet somehow out of the millions and millions of Web sites in cyberspace, you landed on that very one because you were meant to find it. And maybe there are others out there looking for it, too."

Others…like him?

Claudia turned on the rock to face him. Her eyes were bright with excitement, her cheeks pink from the cold. Jack thought she had never looked prettier. "I hate to badger you," she said, "but if you could bring yourself to tell me some of things you've remembered, maybe it'll help figure all this out."

"What do you want to know?"

"Tell me about the Facility. How long were you there? Since childhood?" Her voice was soft with compassion.

He shook his head. "My situation was different from the others. I was raised by a man that I was told was my uncle. The only name I ever knew him by was Ken. We were instructed to call him Uncle, though after a while we realized he was no relation."

"We?"

"My twin brother and I."

Claudia reacted in shock. "You have a twin brother? Where is he?"

"His name is Jared and I don't know where he is."

"Jared." She murmured the name as she digested his

revelation. "So how did you and your brother come to be raised by this Uncle Ken person?"

"Our parents were killed in a car crash when we were five years old, and he showed up out of the blue to take us in."

"But if he wasn't a relative, why did the courts award him custody?"

"I doubt the court was ever involved. A man like that has a way of making things happen, legally or otherwise. Mostly, he just takes what he wants."

She shivered as a chilly breeze swept down from the mountains. "What happened after he took you in?"

"For a long time, we lived with him in his home somewhere in the mountains. It was very secluded and we were never allowed to leave without our 'handlers.' Most of the time we were left alone, and when we got bored, we'd sometimes sneak into the tutor's room and watch his videos. He had a collection of old television shows, but they were new to us and pretty much our only connection to the outside world."

"How long did you live there?"

"Until we were in our teens. As we matured, certain traits began to develop. For me, precognition. For my brother, telepathy. I suppose traces of those abilities were always present, which is why he was interested in us. And why he got rid of our parents."

"He killed them?" She put her hand over his. "My God."

He looked away as an image drifted back to him. A

woman and man were laughing and singing as two little dark-haired boys leaned across the picnic table to blow out the candles on a birthday cake.

Don't forget to make a wish, Jackie, the woman said in his ear as she tickled his ribs. He could smell her perfume. It was a happy scent, like flowers and sunshine.

And then the image faded, replaced by another memory. *Your mother's dead, son, and so is your dad. But don't you worry. I intend to take real good care of you and your brother. You'll be like my own sons. There's nothing to worry about. Nothing at all.*

"I'm so sorry, Jack."

"It was all a long time ago."

"But it's just now coming back. So for you, those memories are fresh and they're bound to be painful. It's okay to be sad," she said softly. "It's best just to let it out."

Her hand was still on his. He waited a moment, then slipped his away. Not because he didn't want her comfort, but because he wasn't sure he could afford it. There was still too much to do and danger was all around them.

She sat quietly, watching him. "Why did you get taken to the Facility?"

"I'd started having visions of what he had in store for us so Jared and I escaped. We were gone for nearly a week before one of his goons found us. A man we called Red."

Claudia gasped. "As in…"

Their gazes met and he nodded. "I think so."

She shuddered. "What did he do when he found you?"

No need to go into all that, Jack decided. He wasn't sure his memories were all that accurate anyway. He wanted to believe some of the images flashing through his head were still part of a lingering nightmare.

"He took us back to Uncle Ken and we were eventually sent to the Facility. I never knew exactly where the place was located. We were drugged and blindfolded, and the next thing I remember was waking up in a tiny cell-like space."

"A cage."

"That's what we called them, yeah."

"Was your brother there, too?"

"Yes, but I didn't know it at the time. We were kept isolated, then eventually moved into an area with other subjects, some older, some younger. That's when the serious experiments started."

She flinched and her hand on the rock inched toward his, but she didn't touch him. "How long did this go on?"

"I don't know. Years. There wasn't much contact with the outside world. Mostly our only interaction was with the staff, and they made a point of not getting emotionally involved. Then one day I was taken to another part of the Facility. I was placed alone in a room with a small black box and instructed to concentrate on my visions."

"So what you said told me last night is true." There was a breathless quality to her voice that made her seem very young. "You were the pre-cog sending me those messages."

"Somehow I was able to tap into your subconscious, I think. At first, I just wanted you to know I was there. I can't explain how much it meant to me to have contact with someone on the outside..." He trailed off for a moment. "And then I began to pick up on something around you. Negative forces. I tried to warn you. After a few days, the vision, the connection...everything just went black. I didn't know what had happened to you, if you were alive or dead."

"That must be when I ran," Claudia said. "Once I was no longer working with the REGs, our connection was severed."

He nodded. "A few weeks ago, I started having the visions again, only they were stronger this time, clearer. You were in danger. Those negative forces were closing in on you again and there was no one to stop them. No way to save you unless I could somehow get to you first. So Jared and I found a way to get out."

"How?"

"It was during one of the experiments." He gazed down at his hands, saw blood dripping from his fingers and closed his eyes. He wouldn't give her the details. And there was very little he could remember of the aftermath until he'd found himself standing in the middle of the road, facing down her car.

He had no idea what had happened to Jared. At some point, they must have gotten separated, and now the only thing that gave him hope of his brother's safety was the faint communication from the day before.

"Jack?"

He turned.

Her eyes were dark and luminous. Beautiful. So beautiful.

"Thank you for telling me," she said. "Thank you for trusting me."

She slipped her hand over his and this time Jack didn't pull away. Instead, he entwined his fingers with hers and they sat for a very long time, looking out over the valley as their frosty breaths mingled on the cold, clean air.

THAT NIGHT THEY ATE dinner in front of the fire, then toasted marshmallows over the flames the way Claudia's father had once taught her. She had purposefully set out to lighten the mood because the rest of the day had been mostly doom and gloom. She and Jack both had been in a bit of funk after their walk, and the silence had stretched on for hours.

Finally, desperate for a little levity, she'd fixed a quick bite to eat, opened another bottle of wine and broke out the chocolate and marshmallows. Now with her favorite band playing in the background and a nice little buzz from the wine, Claudia began to have some not so nice thoughts about Jack.

Was he or wasn't he?

Had he or hadn't he?

She nibbled on a warm, gooey marshmallow, relishing the chocolate coating, as she watched him. As always the play of light and shadow over his features enthralled her. He had such a wonderful face. Handsome, but not too pretty. Interesting, but not too rugged. Boyish, but not too young.

Innocent, but with an overt sex appeal that could knock a woman's socks off. Her socks, if she'd been wearing any. She held one bare foot up to the flames until her skin tingled from the heat.

Jack skewered a marshmallow and held it over the flame. He put as much effort and concentration into the simple task as he did everything else.

A man of details, Claudia thought with a little shiver.

"You have a little chocolate on your mouth," she murmured.

He licked his bottom lip and Claudia almost groaned aloud. "Here let me." She lifted a napkin, but at the last moment, changed her mind and moved in to whip her tongue over the speck of chocolate at the corner of his mouth. "Hmmm."

She lingered, eyes closed, savoring.

When her lids fluttered open, she found Jack watching her intently. There was something in his gaze, an erotic gleam that set her heart to racing.

"Here," she murmured. "Let's try that again."

She picked up the skewer and caressed his mouth with the melted chocolate, leaving a sweet, delectable trail. He never moved a muscle. Not even when she leaned in and ran her tongue over his bottom lip, then tugged gently with her teeth.

He didn't outwardly move, but she could sense his tension. He was like a tightly coiled spring.

She handed him the spear. "My turn."

He hesitated, his eyes going dark, and then he lifted the marshmallow and ran it back and forth across her lips. Claudia had never experienced anything quite so sensual. The sticky sweetness of the marshmallow. The lusciousness of the chocolate. The erotic texture of Jack's tongue as he worked it slowly across her mouth.

"Like that?"

"Exactly like that," she breathed. She cupped the back of his neck with her hands and pressed her lips to his, dipping her tongue inside his mouth, probing, exploring, searching. It took him only a very brief moment before he responded in kind.

"Either you're a very fast learner," she murmured, "Or you've been holding out on me."

He pulled far enough away to stare down at her. He didn't appear at all unsure of himself, nor overly shy or awkwardly eager. He was a man very much in control of his emotions, and that patience, Claudia found, was very exciting.

"Kiss me again," she whispered.

He did. Very, very thoroughly. He traced the outline of her lips with his tongue, as if lapping up the last of the chocolate, and then explored the deepest recesses of her mouth, as if he couldn't get enough of her.

Easing herself onto her back, Claudia pulled him down with her. The weight of his body on hers made her tremble. *This is good. So good.*

She suddenly realized that Jack had stopped kissing her. She opened her eyes and gazed up at him. "What's wrong?"

"Shouldn't we…get undressed?"

"Excellent idea." She sat up and grabbed the bottom of her sweater, yanking it over her head and then tossing it aside. She smiled seductively as she reached around and unfastened her bra. Soon it met the same fate as her sweater.

Jack's gaze devoured her in the firelight.

"Your turn," she murmured and helped him out of his T-shirt. "I find it easier if we just…take off our own jeans," she said, struggling out of the snug denim.

Jack did likewise and Claudia tried not to stare. His nude body was nothing she hadn't seen before, but there were some subtle—and not so subtle—differences tonight. For one thing, he no longer seemed like a stranger to her, and for another, he was in a state of full arousal.

Yowza.

How had she not noticed *that* before?

Well, to be honest, she *had* noticed. She'd just tried not to dwell on his, uh, formidable assets.

"You're beautiful," he said.

"You are." And she meant it. He was a glorious specimen of manliness. All sinewy and sleek.

She picked up the skewer and touched the still soft chocolate to the tip of her breast. "Shall we try a little here?" she whispered. "And here…" She trailed the chocolate down her stomach, lower and lower…

And then she lay on her back and watched as Jack moved over her. He leaned in and kissed her deeply, then flicked his tongue over the chocolate peak of her breast, skimmed it down her stomach, lower and lower…

He was a very quick study. Or a man with no small amount of instinct.

Claudia shivered and moaned and then rising to her knees, she pushed him back to the floor. "Now you."

She didn't bother with the marshmallow but went straight in for the kill. When she was finished, when he seemed on the verge of a powerful explosion, she slid upward, fitting her body to his.

They began to move. Slowly at first and then more frenzied as the buildup became unbearable. Claudia took his hands and placed them on her hips. He grasped her to him, and as their bodies ground together, she tossed her head back and gave herself up to the release.

His came a second later, and she collapsed on top of him, still a-tingle from her climax.

Neither of them spoke for the longest time, and then Jack said in awe, "That was…"

Yeah, Claudia thought. It so was.

THEY FELL ASLEEP in front of the fire. Or rather, Claudia slept. Jack dozed fitfully. He couldn't shut off the stream of memories that poured through his head. Not even in his nightmares could he get away from them. His parents…his brother…the man who claimed to be their uncle. The scientists, the guards, his fellow inmates. On and on, they paraded through his dreams.

After a while, he gave up on sleep, eased himself away from Claudia and rose. He went into the bathroom, showered and dressed, then let himself out the front door. Hurrying down the porch steps, he strode out into the yard and stood gazing up at the sky. He tried to empty his mind, but the memories wouldn't be banished.

And then, slipping through all that chaos, came a gentle probe.

Jack?

The voice was weak this time. Barely there.

He clutched his temples, pressing down tightly with the heels of his hands. *I'm here. I'm safe.*

Jack? Where are you? Where are you?

I'm here, Jared. I'm with the woman.

But the voice was already starting to fade.

He tried to call it back. *Don't go!*

..danger…

Jared!

…they're coming…

A cold wind blew through the trees as Jack stood

there listening to the night. The leaves rustled, the chimes on Claudia's porch tinkled and in the distance, a night creature howled at the moon.

But inside his head, all was silent.

Chapter Twenty-Two

"Claudia? Wake up."

She threw an arm over her eyes as she struggled up through the cobwebs of sleep.

"You need to wake up," Jack said urgently. "The sun is out. We have to get to the monument."

"Hmmm. Okay." She started to snuggle down under the blanket, but Jack's voice finally penetrated, and she bolted upright, her sleep-filled eyes finding his. "What?" Her gaze shot to the window where the soft bloom of winter sunlight slanted through the glass.

She was already fully awake by this time and processing what needed to be done first. Dressed. She had to get dressed.

"Give me just a minute," she said as she scrambled to her feet and dashed toward the bedroom. It was cold in her room, but she barely noticed as she plucked jeans and a sweater from the closet. Then she pulled on wool socks, boots and grabbed her parka. By the time she came out, Jack had already gone outside. Tucking the revolver into her coat pocket, she hurried to join him.

"You don't think we're too late, do you?" she asked anxiously as she backed the SUV down the drive and wheeled onto the road.

"We're not too late. But we should hurry."

As they sped along the road, Claudia contemplated what they might be rushing into. She wished they had back up, but she wasn't naive enough to think that a call to the police would send reinforcements rushing to the monument. Not unless she could come up with a more plausible story than the truth.

She glanced at Jack. He sat slightly forward, staring out the windshield, game face on. And suddenly, Claudia's anxiety spun away, leaving her with a reel of erotic images on repeat inside her head. Jack's hand on her thigh, his mouth on her breast, the whisper of his breath against her lips…

Maybe you shouldn't be thinking such thoughts at a time like this.

Maybe not, but she couldn't help herself. Last night had been *fierce,* and besides, she was doing everything she could to get them to the monument in record time. She had her foot on the gas, her eyes on the road and a loaded weapon tucked away in her pocket. Her preoccupation with their lovemaking was hardly the worst thing that could happen—

A deer sprinted onto the road, stopped dead, and Claudia had to hit the brakes. She swerved onto the shoulder, missing the animal by inches, and for a breathless moment, she fought the wheel as the tires spun on loose gravel. Then she propelled the car back onto the road, and a glance in the rearview mirror assured her that the deer was unharmed. With two graceful leaps, the animal disappeared into the woods.

Claudia let out a shaky breath. Okay, maybe daydreaming about the previous night's events wasn't such a good idea. Evidently, she couldn't obsess over Jack and drive at the same time.

She slanted him a look from the corner of her eye. He remained completely unruffled, so lost in thought she had to wonder if he was even aware of the near miss.

THE MONUMENT WAS CROWDED with tourists. A mild, sunny day had brought them out in droves. As Claudia and Jack emerged from the Hall of Flags onto the viewing terrace, her gaze immediately connected to the massive sculpture. The scope and precision were breathtaking, and she could hear the excited murmur of the tourists as they lined up at the wall to snap photographs that would never do the faces justice.

Trying to tamp down her nerves, Claudia glanced around the terrace. She spotted several school-age children among the crowd, but not a single one in a blue coat and red cap. Nor, thank goodness, had she seen anyone who didn't look as though they belonged. No one stood out, which could be good or bad, she supposed.

She glanced up at Jack. He'd hardly uttered a word since they left the cabin, and now she couldn't help wondering what was going through his head. Maybe, just maybe, they should have spent a little more time planning this thing. They were hardly prepared to take on an army of bad guys. Maybe not even one or two, since neither of them were armed. She'd had to leave her weapon behind because ever since 9/11, security at most of the national monuments had tightened. The last thing she needed was to be taken into custody for carrying a concealed weapon.

But without her revolver, she felt naked and useless. How were they supposed to stop a kidnapping without weapons? At least Jack could use his precognition to balance the odds, but Claudia had zip.

As if reading her mind, Jack said seriously, "I shouldn't have brought you here."

She quirked a brow. "I'm the one who brought you here, remember? And anyway, we're in this together, right? You said yourself it was up to us to stop the kidnappers and save the boy. So let's do this." Big talk, Claudia thought, but her words rang a little hollow. She was starting to have a few regrets herself. Not because she wouldn't do anything to save that child, but because she really wasn't all that brave. Sure, she'd been running from a brutal killer for the past two years, but the key word there was running. And hiding. Barreling headlong into what might very well turn out to be an ambush was a different matter altogether.

Not wanting to give away her jitters, she thrust her hands into her pockets. "So…how do we go about this?" she asked Jack. "How do we find this kid?"

His gaze swept out over the valley. "We need to go back to the trail. That's where he'll be."

"If you say so," she muttered once again following him down the stairs.

The crowd at the bottom was twice as thick as it had been the day before, and there was a lot more foot traffic on the boardwalk. Claudia tried to figure out if this was a good thing or not. It might make it harder to find the boy, but from a personal standpoint, blending in with a crowd could be advantageous.

They strolled along the shady trail, as if taking the time to observe the monument from various angles. At one of the viewing areas, Jack pulled her aside and they pretended to study the faces while surreptitiously watching the parade of tourists on the walkway.

They were standing at such a degree that Claudia had a full view of Lincoln. As she lifted her hand to shade her eyes, she caught the twinkle in his eyes and said excitedly, "Jack, look! The twinkle! Just like in your vision."

He'd turned away and was studying the boardwalk behind them. Reluctantly, Claudia followed his gaze and her heart catapulted to her throat. There, walking toward them on the trail, with the faces highlighted in the background, was a woman and a boy of about ten. He wore a blue coat and a red cap, and even though they were still some distance away, Claudia could see an uncanny resemblance to Jack's sketch.

"That's him!" she whispered.

"Yes." Slowly, Jack turned and scoured the countryside.

"What are we going to do?" Just as Claudia tore her gaze away, she caught a glimpse of someone in a small group of people who were sauntering along the walkway behind the woman and boy. It was the bald man she'd seen in Rapid City the day before. Maybe his presence was merely a coincidence, but somehow Claudia didn't think that was the case.

She put her hand on Jack's sleeve. "See the bald man in the long black coat? I saw him in town yesterday."

Casually, Jack bent as if to tie his shoe. When he straightened, he said, "Don't stare at him. You'll give us away."

Claudia turned back to the faces. "What are we going to do?"

"You wait here."

"Where are you going? Jack?"

He strode down the walkway toward the woman and boy. When he was halfway between them and Claudia, he froze, spun and his gaze widened as their eyes met. He took a few steps back toward her. Over his shoulder, Claudia saw the bald man break from the crowd and lunge toward the boy.

"Jack!" She pointed behind him. What was he waiting for?

His eyes met hers yet again and he screamed, "Get down!" as he turned and rushed for the boy.

She made an involuntary move toward him just as a shot rang out behind her. A portion of the boardwalk shattered and people started screaming in panic. Claudia dropped to the ground and scurried for cover as she scoured the trail for Jack. She saw the woman and boy. They were cowering at the edge of the trail. The woman had her arms around the child, holding on for dear life. Behind them, the bald man sprinted for the woods.

Claudia finally spotted Jack. He was glancing back at her, and when he saw that she was safe, he turned in pursuit.

Keeping her head down, she scrambled over to the woman and boy. "Are you two all right?"

The woman had the boy wrapped so tightly, Claudia wondered how the poor kid was able to breathe. "Did you see that man? He tried to grab my son—"

Just then, a small army of park rangers descended on the area. Claudia could already hear sirens in the distance. As the rangers set about trying to restore order and safely clear the area, Claudia stayed with the woman and her son. By this time, the initial shock had worn off and now the terrified mother grew hysterical. A ranger saw the commotion and came over to take charge of the situation. Between the woman's sobs and Claudia's explanation, they managed to convince him that the boy needed protection.

Two of the rangers rushed mother and son back along the trail while Claudia followed.

"Miss?"

She turned to find another ranger behind her on the path. The first thing she noticed was how tall the man was, how broad his shoulders were. And then beneath his cap, she saw a few strands of unnaturally red hair.

Heart pumping, she turned to call to the rangers, but the man beside her grabbed her arm and said quietly into her ear, "There's a sharpshooter up in those hills with a rifle trained on the boy's head. Unless you do as I say, that kid's as good as dead."

FROM HIS VANTAGE ON the slope above the trail, Jack watched as Claudia followed the tall man back into the woods. He had on a uniform, but Jack wasn't fooled. He could barely see the man's features from so far away, but he recognized him just the same. His name was Red. He was a killer. And he had Claudia.

Jack tracked them until they were out of sight, and then he rose and took off in the opposite direction.

Chapter Twenty-Three

They had walked for hours it seemed up into the mountains, so far off the beaten track that Claudia doubted even Jack would be able to track them. The air grew thinner and colder, and even though she wore her parka and gloves, Claudia couldn't stop shivering.

Where was he taking her? And why was she following along blindly as though she had no will of her own?

At first, her compliance had been to protect the boy, but the farther they got from the trail, the more frantically Claudia had cast about for a means of escape. She'd tried making a break for it once, but the man had easily overpowered her, twisting her arm behind her back until she'd screamed in agony.

That's when she knew what she was up against. If the memory of Dr. Lasher's mutilated body wasn't a graphic enough reminder, the slow smile of pleasure that had spread across his face at her agony told Claudia all she needed to know about her captor. He was a sadist who got off on inflicting pain.

As they struggled up to the summit, he paused and glanced around. At any other time, Claudia would have been struck by the vista—craggy cliffs, purple-shrouded valleys—but now all she could do was nurse her wounded arm and bide her time.

She lowered herself to the ground and leaned back against a rock, closing her eyes at the shooting pain in her arm. She couldn't tell if it was broken or not, but she suspected it might be.

After the man had searched the area, he came back and knelt in the dirt, eyeing her with utter contempt.

"You've put me to a lot of trouble," he said. "I'm going to enjoy this."

Claudia flattened her hand on the stone. The sharp ridges prickled her skin like a burr, bringing her instantly back into the moment. "Why did you kill Dr. Lasher?"

He shrugged. "He was being uncooperative. Not at all a team player."

"You tortured him," Claudia said hoarsely.

A smile. "A weakness of mine, as you shall soon find out."

"Where are you taking me?"

"You ask a lot of questions," he said. "Questions try my patience."

She moistened her lips and tried another tact. "You don't have to do this, you know. I don't know anything. Dr. Lasher never confided in me. Whatever secrets he had of your…employer, he kept them to himself. I'm not a threat to you."

He gave her an amused look. "Do you think this is all for your benefit? I could have taken care of you that same night. This isn't about you."

"Then what do you want from me?"

"You still don't get it yet, do you?" He got up and walked to the edge of the canyon, glancing down. Claudia measured the distance between them. Could she fling herself at him, knock him off the cliff?

He turned with a smile that set her to trembling. "You're a lab rat, Claudia. A guinea pig just like all the others. You may not have been in a cage for the past two years, but we've tracked your every move."

She tried to mask her terror. "Then why wait until now to make your move?"

"Because like I said, this isn't about you. It's about Jack."

"Jack..." His name came out on a whisper.

"He has powers that even he hasn't fully realized. Only so much can be done in the lab. We needed to observe him in the real world. We needed to find out exactly what he's capable of when he's been pushed to the limit." He walked away from the edge of the cliff and came to kneel again in front of her, so close this time that Claudia imagined she could smell the scent of blood on his hands. "He'll come for you, you know. He's already on his way."

"No," a voice said from behind him. "I'm already here."

The man was still facing Claudia, and she felt a sharp, cold thrill run up the length of her spine at the look of cruel satisfaction on his face.

His hand shot out and he grabbed her, pulling her to her feet as he rose swiftly and twisted the already mangled arm behind her. She bit down hard on her lip to keep from screaming in agony as his other arm wrapped around her throat.

He two-stepped her toward the edge of the cliff. She tried to fight him, but his strength seemed almost supernatural. Her feet dragged along the ground like the boneless limbs of a ragdoll.

Everything that happened after that was a blur. A split second after Jack appeared, the man flung her aside with a brutal laugh. She teetered on the edge of the cliff, arms flailing, her eyes going wide as she met Jack's gaze. She tried to scream his name as she tumbled backward, and for a moment, as her feet left the ground, she seemed suspended in mid-air. Before she could go into a free-fall, Jack caught her arm and she cried out in torment.

Eyes locked, he clung to her.

"Don't let go of me," she pleaded.

"Never."

The man came at Jack then before he could haul her up. Jack was looking at her so he couldn't see the man hovering behind him. Claudia tried to scream a warning, but Jack was ready for him. She hadn't noticed before her revolver in his left hand and now he swung around and fired. The bullet only grazed the man's cheek, but the shock stopped him dead in his tracks.

It was enough to buy them some time. Jack hauled her up and she scrambled away from the edge just as Red flung himself at Jack. The impact nearly sent them both over the cliff, and Claudia gasped in terror as they balanced on the precipice for what seemed an eternity.

Then they hit the ground and rolled toward her. Using her good arm, she pulled herself away and crouched in the dirt, shaking and trying to catch her breath, steady her nerves. She had to somehow get a grip because she needed to help Jack.

Where was her gun? One moment he'd had the revolver in his hand and now it was gone. Claudia cast about frantically for the weapon while the two men locked arms in a life and death struggle.

The redhead had size on his side, but Jack was quicker. And he had the advantage of intuiting the bigger man's every move, although this didn't seem to buy him an advantage. As the fight wore on, Claudia began to realize that Jack wasn't the only one whose special abilities had been maximized to the fullest. The superhuman strength she'd sensed earlier was now on full display.

The bodies on the ground writhed and shifted positions so quickly, Claudia could barely tell who was who. They were both bleeding and covered in dirt, and she could hear the gasping breaths as blow after blow connected.

Her arm throbbed and she had to bite back a wave of nausea as she pulled herself along the ground, searching for the revolver. She saw it then, as sunlight sparked off the metal, and she staggered to her feet and lunged toward her. She grabbed the weapon, locked both hands around the grip and whirled.

What she saw took her breath away. Jack was on his back in the dirt with Red's huge hand clamped around his throat, squeezing and squeezing while Jack pounded helplessly at the man's massive arm. With the other hand, Red reached out and grabbed a rock, lifted it over his head with a grinning snarl.

The gun was steady in Claudia's hands. *Never put your finger on the trigger unless you are prepared to shoot.* Without hesitation, she fired.

The punch of the bullet toppled him backward, but he was instantly on his feet, gazing down at the bloom of blood on his shirt. He glanced up, locked eyes with Claudia and took a step toward her.

She lifted the gun. "Don't move."

Jack got to his feet, eyes still blazing. He moved over beside Claudia.

"What should we do with him?" she asked as the aftershock set in and her hands began to tremble. She clutched the grip even harder.

"Where's Jared?" Jack asked coldly. "Where's my brother?"

The blood was gushing from the man's wound. He swayed dizzily, but somehow remained on his feet. Somehow managed to grin. "He's dead."

Jack started toward him, but Claudia grabbed his arm. "Don't. He's baiting you."

"Shoot him," Jack said.

Claudia glanced at him. Shooting a man to save Jack's life was one thing, but putting a bullet in him in cold blood was quite another. "We have to take him in. He'll have to talk to the authorities to save his own skin. It's the only way, Jack."

Before he had time to argue, the man had propelled himself backward to the edge of the cliff. He stood there for a moment, head turned skyward, eyes closed. Jack rushed toward him, but this time he was too late. Still grinning, the man spread his arms wide and tumbled backward over the cliff.

Chapter Twenty-Four

Special Agent Bill Elliot's brown eyes blazed with anger as he stared at them from across the desk. Claudia might have been more than a little intimidated if she hadn't been sailing so high at the moment on painkillers. She glanced down at the new cast on her arm. Her first broken bone—

"Miss Reynolds? Do you have anything you'd like to add to your statement?"

Why did he make it sound like an accusation? Or was that just her imagination. "Uh, no. Not at the moment."

He turned to Jack. "You say this facility is somewhere underground, somewhere remote but you have no idea where."

"That's right. I've told you everything I remember about the place."

"Which isn't much," the agent said impatiently. "We've been on this guy's trail for years. It would have been helpful if you two had managed to bring him in alive."

"Sorry," Claudia said, although when she remembered the guy's grinning face and what he had done to Dr. Lasher, what he might have done to her and Jack, she couldn't muster up much genuine regret.

Special Agent Elliot handed them each a card. "We suspect this guy was responsible for the abductions in this area. And my guess is, he wasn't working alone. I want to nail these bastards to the wall. If you think of anything else, I don't care how trivial it may seem, you call me. You got that?"

After they left the local police station where Elliot had conducted the interrogation, Claudia let out a breath. "Wow, that was pretty intense." He didn't seem to hear her. "Jack?"

She knew what he was thinking about.

She put a hand on his sleeve. "He could have been lying, Jack."

He glanced down at her with tormented eyes. "What if he wasn't? What if my brother really is dead?"

"Then we'll get through it. Right now, let's just go home."

"Home?"

She squeezed his arm. "You got someplace better to go?"

SOMETHING AWAKENED Jack that night, and he got up from Claudia's warm bed and strode outside in the cold.

The night was clear and crisp, and as he stood with his head upturned to the starry sky, he emptied his mind and waited.

It was a long time before he felt the soft probe inside his head, the whisper of a thought that was like the stroke of a feather.

Jack?

Nothing else came through. Whether he'd actually heard his brother's voice or it was merely wishful thinking on his part, Jack had no idea. He stood in the cold for the longest time, unwilling to sever whatever fragile connection might still exist between him and his twin.

"Jack?"

It was Claudia's voice he heard this time, calling softly to him from the porch.

He turned. She stood on the top step, shivering in her diaphanous nightgown. Starlight sprinkled down between them as the wind chimes stirred on the porch. The night suddenly seemed magical. Who better to believe in the impossible than he?

Claudia came down the steps and crossed the yard toward him. He met her halfway and wrapped his arms around her.

"My brother is still alive," he whispered against her hair. "He's out there somewhere and I have to find him."

She drew back, gazing up at him. "Then you will. You found me, didn't you?"

"I had no choice," he said.

"Nor did I, as it turns out." She reached up and trailed her fingertips down his cheek. "I'm here because of you."

He caught her hand and brought it to his lips. "I am because of you."

* * * * *

MAXIMUM MEN continues online
in January 2010!
And don't miss the next
Harlequin Intrigue book in this
heart-stopping continuity when
POWERHOUSE by Rebecca York
goes on sale in February 2010!

Celebrate 60 years of pure
reading pleasure with Harlequin®!
Just in time for the holidays,
Silhouette Special Edition® is proud to
present New York Times *bestselling author*
Kathleen Eagle's
ONE COWBOY, ONE CHRISTMAS

Rodeo rider Zach Beaudry was a travelin' man—until he broke down in middle-of-nowhere South Dakota during a deep freeze. That's when an angel came to his rescue....

"Don't die on me. Come on, Zel. You know how much I love you, girl. You're all I've got. Don't do this to me here. Not *now*."

But Zelda had quit on him, and Zach Beaudry had no one to blame but himself. He'd taken his sweet time hitting the road, and then miscalculated a shortcut. For all he knew he was a hundred miles from gas. But even if they were sitting next to a pump, the ten dollars he had in his pocket wouldn't get him out of South Dakota, which was not where he wanted to be right now. Not even his beloved pickup truck, Zelda, could get him much of anywhere on fumes. He was sitting out in the cold in the middle of nowhere. And getting colder.

He shifted the pickup into Neutral and pulled hard on the steering wheel, using the downhill slope to get her off the blacktop and into the roadside grass, where she shuddered to a standstill. He stroked the padded dash. "You'll be safe here."

But Zach would not. It was getting dark, and it was already too damn cold for his cowboy ass. Zach's battered body was a barometer, and he was feeling South Dakota, big time. He'd have given his right arm to be climbing into a hotel hot tub instead of a brutal blast of north wind. The right was his free arm anyway. Damn thing had lost altitude, touched some part of the bull and caused him a scoreless ride last time out.

It wasn't scoring him a ride this night, either. A carload of teenagers whizzed by, topping off the insult by laying on the horn as they passed him. It was at least twenty minutes before another vehicle came along. He stepped out and waved both arms this time, damn near getting himself killed. Whatever happened to *do unto others?* In places like this, decent people didn't leave each other stranded in the cold.

His face was feeling stiff, and he figured he'd better start walking before his toes went numb. He struck out for a distant yard light, the only sign of human habitation in sight. He couldn't tell how distant, but he knew he'd be hurting by the time he got there, and he was counting on some kindly old man to be answering the door. No shame among the lame.

It wasn't like Zach was fresh off the operating table—it had been a few months since his last round of repairs—but he hadn't given himself enough time. He'd lopped a couple of weeks off the near end of the doc's estimated recovery time, rigged up a brace, done some heavy-duty taping and climbed onto another bull. Hung in there for five seconds—four seconds past feeling the pop in his hip and three seconds short of the buzzer.

He could still feel the pain shooting down his leg with every step. Only this time he had to pick the damn thing up, swing it forward and drop it down again on his own.

Pride be damned, he just hoped *somebody* would be answering the door at the end of the road. The light in the front window was a good sign.

The four steps to the covered porch might as well have been four hundred, and he was looking to climb them with a lead weight chained to his left leg. His eyes were just as screwed up as his hip. Big black spots danced around with tiny red flashers, and he couldn't tell what was real and what wasn't. He stumbled over some shrubbery, steadied himself on the porch railing and peered between vertical slats.

There in the front window stood a spruce tree with a silver star affixed to the top. Zach was pretty sure the red sparks were all in his head, but the white lights twinkling by the hundreds throughout the huge tree, those were real. He wasn't too sure about the woman hanging the shiny balls. Most of her hair was caught up on her head and fastened in a curly clump, but the light captured by the escaped bits crowned her with a golden halo. Her face was a soft shadow, her body a willowy silhouette beneath a long white gown. If this was where the mind ran off to when cold started shutting down the rest of the body, then Zach's final worldly thought was, *This ain't such a bad way to go.*

If she would just turn to the window, he could die looking into the eyes of a Christmas angel.

* * * * *

Could this woman from Zach's past get the lonesome cowboy to come in from the cold...for good?
Look for
ONE COWBOY, ONE CHRISTMAS
by Kathleen Eagle
Available December 2009
from Silhouette Special Edition®

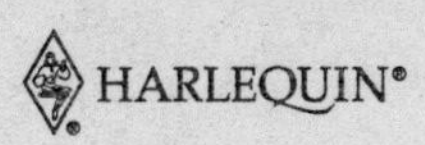

INTRIGUE®

COMING NEXT MONTH

Available December 8, 2009

#1173 FIRST NIGHT by Debra Webb
Colby Agency
To prove his innocence, a talented artist caught up in a murder investigation is in a race against time to catch the true killer—with the help of a Colby agent. And if they can survive the first night, their growing attraction may have a chance as well.

#1174 HIS SECRET CHRISTMAS BABY by Rita Herron
Guardian Angel Investigations
He returns to his hometown determined to forget the past, but a missing child—and the child's adoptive mother—calls out the P.I.'s protective instincts. Can he save the family he never dreamed he'd have?

#1175 SCENE OF THE CRIME: BRIDGEWATER, TEXAS by Carla Cassidy
The small-town Texas sheriff has enough on his hands with a killer on the loose, but the feisty FBI profiler who insists on being a part of the case—against his wishes—may just be the woman he needs....

#1176 BEAUTY AND THE BADGE by Julie Miller
The Precinct: Brotherhood of the Badge
When the girl next door blows the whistle on illegal activities at work, the only person she can turn to for protection is her gruff cop neighbor—a man who is ready, willing and able to be her true-blue hero.

#1177 SECLUDED WITH THE COWBOY by Cassie Miles
Christmas at the Carlisles'
After rescuing his wife from a kidnapper, the cowboy is determined to seal the rift between them and remind her of their love. But when she comes under threat again, his actions may speak louder than words as he fights to save what's his.

#1178 POLICE PROTECTOR by Dani Sinclair
When she discovers that her sister and her sister's children are missing, a career-minded businesswoman turns to a take-charge detective to find them—and as he takes on the dangerous case, he shows her that family is what matters most....